MW00958819

BY SIN TO ATONE

A FORCED PROXIMITY SECRET SOCIETY
ROMANCE

SINNERS DUET
BOOK 1

NATASHA KNIGHT

ABOUT THIS BOOK

I crossed him. Now he owns me.

When I tried to blackmail Ezekiel St. James, I thought it would be easy.

But I had no idea who I was dealing with.

The moment his steel-grey eyes locked on mine, I knew the game was over.

He knew exactly who I was. What I'd done.

And he wasn't going to let me walk away.

With his immense wealth and power, he had me kidnapped.

He could make me disappear.

I'm no easy prey, though, and it's not just my life on the line. I have to protect my sister.

But when I'm hurt, he does the unexpected. He takes care of me.

In some twisted way, he sees his atonement in me.

Desperate and vulnerable, I need protection. He offers his, but it will come at a cost.

His terms are as grey as his morals. I'll be his in every way.

But when he touches me, my skin catches fire.

And there's something inside me that wants to belong to him.

NOTE FROM THE AUTHOR

The *Sinners Duet* is set in the world of *The Society* (officially known as IVI) and tells the story of Ezekiel St. James. We first meet Ezekiel in the *Devil's Pawn Duet*, but you can read *The Sinners Duet* without having read any other books in this world.

IVI

Imperium Valens Invictum

The story you are about to enjoy is set in the world of *The Society* created by A. Zavarelli and Natasha Knight. Although you do not need to read any other books to follow this story, here is a brief description of what IVI is and how it operates.

Imperium Valens Invictum, or IVI for short, is Latin for

Strong Unconquered Power. The organization is frequently referred to by its members as The Society.

We are a well-established organization rooted in powerful dynasties around the world. Some call us thieves in the night. A criminal syndicate. Mafia. The truth is much more intricate than any of those simplistic terms.

Our ancestors learned long ago there was power in secrecy. The legacy handed down to us was much more evolved than that of the criminals waging war on each other in the streets. We have money. We have power. And we are much more sophisticated than your average knee-breaking Italian mob boss.

IVI holds its members in the highest regard. With that power comes expectation. Education. Professionalism. And above all, discretion. By day, we appear as any other well-bred member of society. They don't and never will know the way our organization operates.

Thirteen families founded the ancient society. These families are held in the highest regard and referred to as the Upper Echelon. These are the Sovereign Sons and Daughters of The Society.

The Society has its own judicial branch, The Tribunal, that operates outside the norms of what is acceptable in the world today. Its laws are the final law for Society members.

The Society will go to great lengths to protect its members from the outside world but their expectations are often higher and sentences handed down from The Tribunal often harsher if even, at times, Medieval.

Welcome to The Society...

PROLOGUE
EZEKIEL

I know what you did.

Ice clinks against the crystal tumbler. I lift it to my mouth and sip the whiskey but don't quite taste it. Don't quite feel the numbing effects of it.

I read the text message for the hundredth time, tempted to reply, angrily staring at my screen as if it will give me an answer. A name. A fucking face.

I know what you did.

That's it. Five words accompanied by a newspaper article about the accidental death of my father and his mistress.

Mother. Fucker.

"Mr. St. James?" a woman's soft, slightly accented voice interrupts.

I shift my gaze up to the server who clears her throat, a blush already creeping along the pale skin of her neck.

Nora.

I check my expression, force a smile.

"Yes, Nora?"

"The gentleman you were expecting is here to see you, sir."

I glance at my wristwatch and nod to her. That pink hue blooms, coloring her cheeks. She's sweet. Young. Pretty. Very pretty. And far too inexperienced for her own good. There's a part of me that knows I should warn her. Tell her to stay away from the men who frequent this club. Men like me. But I'm too selfish for that. And nowhere near good enough to do it.

"Show him to my table."

"Yes, sir."

"And make sure we're not interrupted, will you?"

"Yes, sir." She turns to go, hesitates.

"What is it, Nora?" I ask, trying to keep the impatience from my tone.

"Um. I was wondering if you'd perhaps need me later?" she asks, a note of optimism in her voice even as she swallows the last part.

That pink deepens to crimson. She's embarrassed.

"You're sweet to ask, but no. Not tonight," I say.

She blinks, looks every which way but at me. "Oh. I..." She finally clears her throat and is able to meet my gaze once more. "I'm sorry, I just—"

"Let's not keep my guest waiting, Nora. You know how I feel about being made to wait."

"Yes, sir. Of course, sir." She nearly trips in her rush to get to the door. I don't even watch her go. I look at my phone instead. At that fucking message that has stolen the little joy I have these days. But when I hear the overly exaggerated twang that can only belong to Robbie Shetland, I tuck the phone into my pocket and watch him enter, charming Nora. He towers over her with his big cowboy boots, the signature fur coat he inherited from his granddaddy, as he likes to tell the story, the black hat still on his head. He catches my eye but there's no break in his monologue.

The other patrons turn to take in the large, loud American who clearly doesn't belong. Eden 9.5 is a high-end bar known for its many shadowy corners. It's tucked in an out-of-the-way alley in Amsterdam's Red Light District. Hidden in plain sight, it doesn't draw the multitude of tourists who frequent the district.

Robbie tips his hat to someone whose eye he catches, and I study the way he makes himself appear so casually unaware. So fucking clueless and not at all like the man he is. In reality, I am sure he's cataloged all the faces in this room already. He has that kind of memory. I'm certain he will know all their names by tomorrow morning.

I stand, adjust a shirtsleeve. The polished Montblanc cufflink gleams when it catches the light.

"Robbie," I say, stepping around the small table. I extend my hand in greeting. "Pleasure to see you again."

He shakes my hand. "Pleasure's all mine," he says, then turns to Nora. "Truly. All the pleasure is mine." He bends to kiss the inside of her wrist and I almost roll my eyes.

"Nora if you'll take Mr. Shetland's coat and hat?" I ask.

"Yes, sir," she says as Robbie slips his coat off and hands both it and his hat to her.

"You take good care of that, sweetheart," he says with a wink.

"I will, sir. Can I bring you anything else?" she asks, but there's a bottle of whiskey and a second tumbler already waiting on the table.

"Looks like I've got everything I need."

Nora nods, turns and walks away.

Robbie watches her go. "Sweet little piece."

"Inexperienced," I tell him.

"Lucky for her, I'm a very patient teacher." He settles into the chair across from mine.

I take my seat. "Remind me again why you make such a spectacle of yourself," I say, pouring Robbie a whiskey before picking up my glass and leaning back in the deep, comfortable leather chair.

He glances around the room. Most of the patrons have resumed their conversations although a few still glance his way. He smiles, says a howdy to one, gaze steady. The man who was looking down his nose at Robbie clears his throat and turns away.

"Don't know what you mean. I'm just a loud American tourist," he says to me, sipping his drink.

"Right."

He shrugs. "Better for me if everyone thinks I am at least. Easier, considering my line of work."

He's right about that. Robbie Shetland is one of the most cunning men I know. He came from nothing, no, less than nothing. His mother and sister probably cleaned toilets for men like those sitting here tonight. The elite of the elite with more money and privilege than brains. And he has a way of finding people who don't want to be found. He's known within The Society. Although not a member himself, he has worked privately for several members. It's one of the reasons we're meeting here tonight and not at a Society venue. I don't want anyone knowing my business.

"What do you have for me?" I ask.

He takes a single, folded sheet of paper out of his pocket. It's crumpled and he makes a point of setting it on the table and flattening out the creases.

"It's fine." I pick it up and when I see what's on it, I raise my eyebrows. "What the hell am I supposed to do with this?" It's some sort of computer-generated code I can't make heads or tails of.

"That piece of paper tells us where those emails originated."

I glance again at the sheet as he points out a couple of things and starts explaining.

"I don't want a lesson in reading code. That's why I hired you. I just need the answers."

"I'm getting to it. You ready for this?" He pauses for dramatic effect. "The email you received originated from New Orleans."

"What?" I ask. Judging from the look on his face, the shock must be evident on mine.

"From an unremarkable little apartment in a part of town I'm sure you, being Society folk, don't frequent."

"New Orleans?" Dread claws my gut.

"Oh, forgot one more thing." He digs around in his pockets and takes out another crumpled piece of paper. "Here she is." He unfolds the sheet and hands it to me. "Coincidence of coincidences, turns out she's an employee of The Cat House."

I take it from him. It's a grainy, black and white printout on cheap paper.

"The Cat House? As in, The Society Cat House?"

"One and the same. Hell of a coincidence."

"And it's a woman?" I try to make my eyes focus on the page, take in the shoulder-length dark hair, the big eyes on the woman's unsmiling face.

"Women do blackmail. We live in modern times. Equal opportunity and all that."

I shift my gaze back to him. "You sure this is correct? If she works at the Cat House—"

"Not in the way you think." He winks, chuckles while shaking his head. "Dirty devil. She serves drinks."

I look again at the sheet of paper. "This is the best photo you could come up with?"

He shrugs a shoulder. "Hotel's printer was nearly out of ink."

I study the printout more closely. "How old is she?" she barely looks to be eighteen.

"Twenty-seven according to her ID."

"Right." This girl is not twenty-seven. It's a fake, obviously. "What do you know about her?"

"Her name, well, I should say the name she gave HR, do you all have HR?" he asks, pausing. I raise my eyebrows. "I digress. The name she gave whoever hired her is Blue Masterson. She doesn't have a social media profile, no on-line presence at all, in fact. Very odd especially for someone her age. That there is her employee mug shot."

I look from the photo to him. "Blue Masterson. Even that sounds fake."

"Blue moved to a shitty little apartment in NOLA about six months ago." Six months. The first email only showed up around two months ago.

"From where?"

"Don't know."

"What do you mean you don't know?"

"No paper trail but I'm still searching."

I look at the picture again. She's attractive. Like all the things that are bad for you are attractive. Her gaze is sharp, clever and cautious in that way people who are hiding something have. I know it well.

"Are you sure it's her?" She just seems too young. Too poor. Too much not a part of the world I come from.

"I don't make mistakes, Zeke."

"Ezekiel." Only my mother, my brother and my niece call me Zeke. Zoë used to. Not sure she'd ever even said my full name.

"Ezekiel. Pardon me."

I blink to clear the memory of Zoë. "It's fine."

"Blue Masterson has managed to erase her past. She's better at it than most which is surprising. Dig as I might, I don't get any hits. Like she didn't exist until she showed up in New Orleans. The only thing I've managed to find are monthly payments to the Oakwood Care Center."

My forehead creases. "What's that?"

"Psychiatric hospital."

"Oh?"

"Don't know more just yet. All that fucking patient privacy and this place actually has decent online security."

I sit back looking at the strange girl's face, her

narrowed eyes. She looks like she's telling off the photographer. "So, she's using a fake name. Fake papers. But if she works at IVI, she'd have been vetted."

He shrugs a shoulder. "If you say so." He finishes the whiskey in his glass and reaches to pour himself another. "I'll be sticking around here a few days. Never been to Amsterdam, you know. But I'm guessing you'll be heading back to New Orleans pronto."

"It appears so."

"I jotted her schedule down on the back of that photo."

I turn it over. "You'll keep looking into Ms. Masterson." I get to my feet, taking out my wallet and dropping some bills onto the table for Nora.

"I wouldn't consider my job done until I figure out who the hell she is."

"I want to know everything there is to know about this woman. Every fucking detail."

"You got it."

"You know how to reach me."

He nods and I turn and walk away.

1

BLUE

24 Hours Later

I sip cold, burnt coffee, and scan my phone, refreshing the screen. Waiting. Still waiting. I should have had the money by now. Actually, Ezekiel St. James should have made the deposit weeks ago. But nothing. I sent another message this morning telling him not to play hard to get. Mentioning going public with my information in an attempt to light a fire under his rich ass. It's not like he doesn't have the money. Hell, a man like him will hardly miss 100K. For me, that money could mean the difference between life and death.

Water hisses on the stove making me jump. I set the phone on the counter and turn off the burner. I don't know why I'm boiling pasta. I'm running late as it is so I'm not going to have time to eat more than a few bites before my shift.

Using a kitchen towel so as not to burn my hands, I lift the pot and hold the lid in place while pouring the steaming water into the sink. I set the pot back on the stove and dig a fork out of the drawer. I stab some of the noodles, cramming them into my mouth straight out of the pot. I can't have my stomach growling as I'm serving the good men of The Society who have come to get their dicks sucked at The Cat House, after all. Not a good look. I eat several more forkfuls as I check the bank account, refreshing my screen yet again. Still no money.

Once I've crammed most of the pasta into my mouth, I check the time and tuck the phone into the pocket of my baggy sweats, the only thing I've got on that's warm and remotely comfortable. I'm wearing the uniform—if you can call it that—that's required for the serving staff of The Cat House. I pulled on a pair of sweatpants over top because it's basically a onesie that rides too far up my ass and is cut so low one wrong move and a boob will pop right out. There's a skirt. Well, it's more a flap of material that leaves about half my butt on display. And somehow, it's supposed to send a message that we're not to be touched. Ogling is okay though. And flipping the skirt up every freaking time I bend over to set a drink down. I swear, they act like a bunch of horny teenagers.

I drop the fork and pot into the sink of the grimy little kitchen in this minuscule apartment and remind myself it's temporary. Besides, even here, I'm lucky. I got off mostly unscathed. I'm much better off than Wren is or will ever be again.

At the thought of my sister, I dig my phone out of my pocket and send a text to Rudy, her main nurse.

He'll get the message to her. It's a knock-knock joke, a game we play. I smile as I type out the words but it's bittersweet because that's pretty much what the entirety of this chat is made of. Stupid knock-knock jokes a child of six would find funny, not a twenty-one-year-old woman.

Shit.

I draw a deep breath in and stare up at the popcorn ceiling to hold back the tears. I can't redo my makeup. I don't have time.

What would she think if she saw me now in this uniform? Or I should say what would the old Wren think? I know what I look like.

Once I'm sure I won't cry, I cross over to the closet to pick up my raincoat. That is an irrelevant question anyway. She'll never see me in this thing. My time at The Cat House is coming to an end, after all. As soon as Zeke pays up. Then I can go get Wren. Drive up to Canada eventually. There's a really good facility there and with that money in my account, I can afford it.

Anyway, that part comes later. I need to get the money first and, in the meantime, I need to keep my job at The Cat House. The patrons do tip well, at least.

I slip my arms through my coat sleeves, grab my purse, and leave the apartment, locking the three locks behind me. The hallway smells, as usual, of fried food, rot and old shoes. It's gross but I hold my breath, hearing the sounds I've become familiar with. A baby crying. Televisions on full blast. Someone yelling. I walk to the end of the hall, down the stairs and out the double glass doors of the crappy apartment building only to stop short when, at the bottom of the stairs, I see a Rolls Royce idling.

My heart leaps to my throat. I nearly throw up when the driver's side door opens and a chauffeur in full uniform steps out. He nods what I guess is meant to be a greeting to me. I stare, eyebrows high as, without a word, he opens the backdoor of the car and gestures for me to get in.

I force a deep inhale. Rain is pouring off his hat, down the long black leather trench. His face is cast in shadow by that hat and his hands are gloved. He's tall, well over six feet.

"Miss," he says when I don't move. "Mr. Craven sent me to make sure you arrive safe and sound."

Well. That's unusual.

"Craven sent you to pick me up?" I ask. Maybe I didn't hear right. Craven, or Creepy Craven as we call him, is the handsy manager of the handful of female servers at The Cat House. It used to only be men who performed the task of bringing drinks to the rich and horny. The women who are employed by the establishment offer a different sort of service.

The driver nods.

Craven is an asshole. I can't wait to tell him as much once Ezekiel St. James pays up and I can get the hell out of New Orleans. There's no way he of all people would care about me getting anywhere safe and sound.

I cock my head and study the driver. "Why would he do that?" I ask. If there's one thing I've learned over the last couple of years it's that you can't trust people.

"Miss, I'm sure Mr. Craven doesn't want you arriving at work drenched." He gestures to the car.

Well, that's a more selfish reason so it makes sense.

I glance at the bus stop across the street just as a car speeds past it, splashing the two people waiting in the shelter. My car, which stands in the far corner of the parking lot, is temperamental at best these days. I'd most likely be standing there with them if it weren't for this guy, so, with a sigh, I walk down the stairs and peer into the backseat. It's empty.

"Okay," I say, and get in. "Thanks, I guess."

The driver closes the door and climbs casually into his seat as if unbothered by the weather. As soon as he puts the car into drive, the locks engage. The sound weirdly makes me jump. I meet the driver's eyes in the rear-view mirror and quickly look away, feeling embarrassed. I focus on putting on my seatbelt instead then settle into the comfortable leather chair. In front of me, on the back of the headrest is the IVI emblem engraved into the leather. I wonder if this is Craven's personal car. No, it wouldn't be. He wouldn't get a company car. But maybe he has one at his disposal. He's not a member of The Society, just staff. Like me. I'm guessing he signed the same NDA I did. But John Craven likes to put on airs and make sure we, the lowly female serving staff, know he's a rung above us in the food chain. Did I mention he's an asshole? It bears repeating.

I shift my gaze to the road and try to relax even as something about this whole thing feels off. I look at the driver again and for a moment wonder if I'm being kidnapped. If I was stupid enough to walk right into some serial killer's car. But we're following the familiar road to the IVI compound. It's fine. I'm fine.

My phone pings. I startle, then reach into my bag to get it. When I see it's a notification about a deposit into my account, my stomach lurches. I'm not sure it's excitement or anxiety, to be honest.

My heart thuds against my chest and I hold my breath as I log into the app to look at the account which up until yesterday had a whopping dollar in it.

Now, it has two.

"What the fuck?" I mutter. I bite my lip and feel the line between my brows deepen as I peer closer. It's got to be some kind of mistake. But no, I'm right. A deposit of a dollar was made just seconds ago. And the reference accompanying it is a middle finger emoji.

"Asshole."

Before I can even begin to think about what to do, how to respond to this, my first communication from Ezekiel St. James, the driver is pulling into the IVI compound.

I drop my phone back into my purse as the Rolls Royce comes to a stop. I push the button to unlock the seatbelt as the driver, not wasting any more of his breath on me, opens the door and waits for me to exit. At least we're under the overhang which I'm grateful they have even at the staff entrance because somehow the rain is even worse now.

I climb out, rush into the building that houses The Cat House and slip into the lady's locker rooms. A glance at the clock tells me I'm a few minutes late so I hurry to slip off the sweats and shove them into my locker, taking out the stiletto heels and swapping out my ancient sneakers for them. Once I'm in uniform, I dig my phone out again and check that deposit, sure it's not right. But it's right there. A whole dollar was deposited into my account.

Was it a mistake?

No. The emoji confirms that.

So, what now? What do I do? Go public? With what exactly? It's not like I have solid evidence. No smoking gun. What I found on my dad's laptop would definitely lead people to ask questions but for a man as wealthy as Ezekiel St. James, he could probably cover anything up.

This isn't how this is supposed to go. He's meant to think I can damage him, and he's just supposed to pay.

The locker room door swings open, making me jump.

Ed walks in.

"Jesus, Ed. You almost gave me a heart attack!" I drop the phone back into my purse and close the locker.

Ed is one of the bouncers. Well, they prefer to be referred to as security guards. Eyeroll. The Society is too posh to call them bouncers. But men are men wherever you go, and where there is money, liquor and sex on offer, things inevitably get out of hand, so I get it. It's just that more often than not, they seem to be on our ass rather than the men who step out of line.

"Blue, let's go."

"Coming." I grab the choker from inside my purse and clasp it around my neck. Part of the 'uniform'. A collar with a clasp at the front. Just for looks, or so they tell us. The courtesans wear them too, and I've seen the men make use of theirs.

I walk over to the mirror to make sure the ring is just above the hollow between my collarbones and remind myself no one can actually touch me. I serve drinks. That's all.

Ed clears his throat. I ignore him and secure the few hairs that have fallen out of the bun at the nape of my neck. After checking my carefully applied makeup doesn't need a touch-up, I hurry toward the club. Craven already has an issue with my hair, of which the topmost layer is sapphire blue, and underneath is my natural black. I dyed it when we got to New Orleans. Not sure why I did it, actually. It's not as though it helps me to blend in. The opposite. But I needed to hold on to some part of myself. Have some control. Being on the run, you can forget who you are. You can give the people you're running from power over you. Maybe it was just my fuck you to my father, Tommy, or as he likes to be called, Lucky Tommy. Fucking asshole. If he'd just stayed gone, if mom hadn't taken him back when he came crawling, everything would be different.

As I slip under Ed's arm, he whistles. I flip him off because I can. I hear the soft classical background noise and a woman's giggle before I even enter the bar. Craven is standing at the opposite end ogling one of the courtesans who is kneeling at the feet of a member as he attaches a leash to her collar. He then leads her to a private room. She's on her hands and knees, her ass on display. Craven will most likely jerk off to the sight of it as soon as he has a free moment. He earned the nickname Creepy after all. When he shifts his gaze to me, he narrows his eyes and makes a point of tapping his watch.

Yeah, I know I'm late, asshole. Can I blame his driver?

"Table six," the bartender tells me, setting two whiskeys on a tray and pushing it toward me before turning to fill the next order.

I grab the tray and, keep my gaze on one point on the far wall in order not to fall over on my toothpick thin heels, another requirement of the uniform. I cross the room toward table six and try not to see what is happening in my periphery. Alcoves and rooms are offered to members for privacy, but I swear the men who frequent the place like to be watched. Sadly, most are pathetic to look at.

But as I approach my table, I paste on a smile, thinking of the tips, because based on that single dollar deposit and the middle finger emoji, Zeke won't be paying up and I'm back to square one.

That's one thing about members of The Society. They tip generously. If you lean deep while pouring their drinks and make sure to swing your ass when you walk away, even better. The two at my table don't have women with them. I'm at least grateful for that. It's always a little uncomfortable when they do. But they're both wearing their masks and cloaks. It's not unusual but by the time I get to my shift which starts at midnight, most men have shed both. Behind the closed doors and within the windowless rooms of the establishment, what happens at The Cat House stays at The Cat House.

The two stop their conversation as I approach, turning their gazes to me. Something about the action or the two sets of eyes on me, makes me hesitate.

I misstep.

The ringing in my ears starts, a warning.

An omen.

No. It's not that. It's the cloaks and masks. It'd make any woman nervous, but I remind myself it's just grown men essentially wearing costumes, playing some stupid game.

I close my eyes and tell myself to relax. If I just breathe, I can get through it. It will pass. It always does.

When the high-pitched beep lessens, I tamp down the nausea that accompanies it and adjust my grip on the tray. My palms are sweaty. I return my gaze to the men, telling myself to calm down as my lips quiver in my attempt to smile. They both watch me and neither of them smiles. One, I realize, has one dark eye and one gray eye. It's unusual but it's the other man, the one whose head is slightly tilted, whose wolfish eyes burn a bright, almost unnatural silver-gray, who holds my attention. Who makes me aware of how loudly my heart beats against my chest.

A shiver runs down my spine, making all the hairs on the back of my neck stand on end. I reach the table and nod my greeting because I don't think my voice will work. They still don't return my smile. They just keep staring at me and that same feeling of earlier, of something being off, returns.

Bending down, I set their drinks before them. I take a minute to close my eyes and force another deep breath in. I'm fine. Everything is fine. It's just been a weird night. I'm distracted and I need to figure out what I'm going to do next, that's all, because Ezekiel St. James's response tells me he's not going to pay. What my dad had on him, it's not as big a deal as he thought, maybe. Blackmail isn't how my dad made his money, not his real money anyway. He's more of a bully than anything else.

When I straighten and look up, my gaze collides with the silver-eyed man and that ringing starts again, causing me to lose my balance and stumble backward. The tray drops from my hand, hitting the table loudly on its way to the plush carpet at our feet.

The man is on his feet lightning fast, hands closing over my elbows searing my skin. His grip is just a little too tight as he rights me.

I look up at him, instinctively wrapping my hands around his forearms as the ground seems to tilt beneath my feet. It's not real. I know that. It's just my broken brain. So, I hold on until it passes, and I stare into those strange wolf-eyes that have stolen my voice. My breath. It's the way he's looking at me, like he sees right through me, that sends my heart catapulting against my ribs, blood thudding against my ears as the room spins around us.

Danger.

The word manifests as pure sensation, a visceral knowledge.

When I'd felt like something was off earlier, that wasn't nothing. Don't I know to trust my instincts yet? It was a premonition. Something coming. Something bad. And that sensation is amplified a thousand times in this stranger's eyes.

"Gentlemen. Everything all right?" Craven's voice comes from behind me. The man who has hold of me doesn't break eye contact. I wish he would so I could breathe. Wish he'd loosen his hold so I could slip away.

"Craven," the one who was seated, who is now standing, says. "Everything is fine." He turns to the man who has me, sets his hand on his shoulder. I look at it and see the curving line of dark ink tattooed into his skin, the scaly tail of some creature inked on his arm? It disappears under the sleeve of his shirt.

"Blue can be clumsy." Craven closes a meaty hand around my bare arm and nausea twists my gut. I hate when he touches me.

The silver-eyed man shifts his gaze from me to Craven's hand to his face and a coldness, more icy than moments ago, settles into those storm-angry eyes. He doesn't say a word. Doesn't need to. Not a moment later, Craven removes his sweaty paw from my shoulder and the masked man who has hold of me releases me. The instant he does, I put space between us, bending to pick up my tray, pushing strands of hair that's fallen out of my bun back behind my ears.

"She didn't spill anything on you, did she, Mr. St. James?"

Mr. *What*?

The world tilts and it takes all I have not to topple over.

"She'll be reprimanded if she did," Craven is saying. He mutters something about borrowing a cane and laughs like it's the funniest thing anyone has ever said. He's the only one laughing.

Get your shit together, Blue. Get it fucking together. Even if he's him, he doesn't know who I am. He has no idea. How could he?

"Excuse me," I manage.

The man with the wolf eyes settles into the oversized leather armchair and picks up his tumbler of whiskey. When his sleeve draws back, I catch a glimpse of the expensive watch on his wrist and ink similar to the other man's twisting around to the back of his hand. I wonder what it is. Why they both have it and what it means. And I'm reminded this is for real. Not a game.

Ezekiel St. James is a member of a secret society and I tried to blackmail him.

When my gaze flitters up to his, I find his locked on me, watching me. Not missing a single beat.

Fingers on my throat, I slip away as quickly as I can, hearing Craven make some apology offering to comp their drinks. I push through the swinging doors of the locker room and run into a bathroom stall where I lock the door behind me, drop to my knees and puke.

2

EZEKIEL

Craven finally walks away. This round of drinks is on him apparently. Fucking idiot.

The curtain the girl disappeared behind settles into place. From the look on her face, I guess she heard who I was.

"I take it that's her," Jericho says. I feel his eyes on me as he slips his mask to the top of his head. "You okay?"

I swallow whiskey, feeling more okay than I have since receiving the first email months ago. In fact, I feel anger, only anger. I push my mask off and turn to Jericho.

"I'm fine. Good, actually."

"Are you going to tell me what the hell is going on?"

My brother and I study one another. It's been three years since I've seen him. We've talked a handful of times in those years. Business mostly. He looks good. Younger somehow. Happy.

"How is your wife?" I ask, instead of answering his question, because I know she's one of the reasons he's happy.

He smiles, warmth blooming in his eyes. Something new for my brother. "Isabelle's good."

"Angelique?"

"Getting bigger every day. She misses you, you know."

"We FaceTime often." Angelique is my niece. She's Jericho and Kimberly's daughter whom Jericho kept hidden from the world for years. Hidden from me, too. I understood his decision. I'd probably have done the same, considering.

"FaceTime is not the same and you know it."

"Mom and the boys?" My brother adopted Matty Bishop, Isabelle's nephew, the son of his enemy. He and Isabelle had their first child, a boy named Christian, a year and a half ago and their second son, Adan, a few months ago.

"They're all good. You should see Angelique with them. Calls them the kids." He chuckles. It's a new look for my brother. It's a good look. "And mom's doing well. Healthy. Happy." He pauses. "Isabelle's pregnant again," he adds, seeming almost hesitant. Almost as though he is not sure if he should share his news with me. "A happy surprise."

"Contraception is a thing, brother."

He shrugs a shoulder.

I smile. I'm happy for him, truly. I want to be, at least. Although there's something between Jericho and I that has never healed. That I seem to hold on to. Seeing him again after these years just reminds me how powerful that thing is.

Jericho is my big brother and in the years Zoë, mom and I needed him most, he was gone. Traveling to whatever corner of the world he wanted to disappear to while the shitstorm that was our father ripped our home, and what was left of our family, apart. It may be unfair, but I can't help but wonder if things might have been different if Jericho hadn't left whenever he could. If he'd just been there with us. He knew what dad was like even if he didn't know everything he'd done until it was far too late. But, when things got ugly, Jericho vanished without once looking back. I haven't forgiven him, even if there's a part of me that wants to. That knows he was dealing with things the only way he knew how.

Jericho's face darkens. I assume it matches mine because the air between us has shifted palpably.

"Why is your return a secret, Zeke?" he asks.

I asked him to meet me here, only calling him from the airport once I landed in New Orleans. I hadn't decided up until then if I'd tell him I was back in town. I'm not planning on staying long. Just until I take care of Blue Masterson or whatever the hell her name is. But in order to do that, I need him.

I glance around, making sure we can't be overheard. We're sitting in the farthest corner of the club and the others are preoccupied. I reach into my jacket pocket and retrieve my phone. Scrolling down my email, I open the first message I received from Blue Masterson and turn it, so the screen faces him.

Jericho reads it and I watch his face harden. He reaches for the phone, takes it, and opens the attachment which is a newspaper article reporting the deadly crash.

Our father, along with one of his many mistresses, was killed in a car accident in Austria several years ago.

For a long time, only I knew it wasn't an accident. Jericho pieced the puzzle together and confronted me more recently. It was only after that he learned why I did it.

My chest tightens at the thought of why I did what I did. I wonder if this pain is so acute even now, so many years after Zoë's death, because we were so close once. So close we shared our mother's womb. We were twins. That bond between us, that connection, it faded as we grew older, but I still remember the feeling of having a second half. A part that was not me but so much a part of me that I still feel the loss of her. I remember the comfort that bond brought me, even when I was too young to put words to it. The pain of losing her, and the way I lost her, it's a heavy, solid thing that is unchanging. Unending.

It is pain. Just pain.

Jericho looks back at me, a furrow between his brows, his eyes narrowed with fury.

"How long have you been sitting on this?"

"Couple months."

"Months? And *she* sent this?" he gestures toward the curtain Blue disappeared behind.

I nod.

"You're sure?"

"I have a reliable source." I drink another sip of whiskey and take my phone back.

"How would she have found out?" The evidence Jericho had to put the pieces together was footage from the hotel I'd stayed in while doing what I needed to do when I was in Austria. There is nothing that puts me at the scene of the crime because as far as the world knows, there was no crime. The car and its occupants were burnt up so badly there was no physical evidence to investigate.

I wonder if he died on impact. It's how the coroner said it would have happened considering the cliff they drove off. I hope it wasn't instantaneous. Not for him. I hope he felt fear followed by the pain of a fiery death. I hope it lasted and lasted while he burned and burned.

"Zeke," Jericho calls me into the present.

I grit my teeth, darkness at the thought of the past settling in my gut. I swallow back the pain, the emotion, the guilt. Not guilt over the murder of my father. No. Guilt for the loss of Zoë. For what she endured. For my being absent to her just as I blame Jericho for being absent from us.

"Yeah?" I ask, eyes narrowed, heart rate settled, any emotion locked back up.

"What does she know exactly and how does she know it?"

"That's what I'm going to find out."

"There's no evidence."

I raise my eyebrows in question.

Jericho draws a tight breath in. "How are you going to find out?"

"The Bishop house is still empty?" Matty inherited the Bishop house which is part of Jericho's property now. Once he is of age, he'll come into his inheritance, which includes the house.

Jericho nods. "It's closed up. Been that way since Bishop was killed."

"It's private then."

He nods again. "I can have someone go out there. Open it up for you."

"I don't want anyone to know I'm here. Not yet."

He lifts his chin, studies me in that way he has, the silence drawn out just a little longer than necessary. He disagrees with this part.

"If I need to take care of things..." I trail off, unsure myself how far I'm willing to go to keep my secret. To keep Zoë's. I've killed twice. I am capable. Maybe that's what worries my brother.

He shifts his gaze once more to the curtain from which Blue Masterson has yet to emerge. I watch Jericho. His hands aren't exactly squeaky clean. His past is possibly more violent than mine. At least up until this point.

"You're sure it's her? I mean, before you do anything you need to be sure."

"I am."

He studies me for a beat, then nods. "The house is yours to use, you know that." He digs his phone out, types something and my phone pings. "First one is the code for the gate. Second one will get you into the house."

"Thank you."

"What's your plan exactly?"

"I want to find out what she knows. Who she's talked to if anyone. I also want to know who the hell she really is because she's not who she's pretending to be." I hear the built-up fury in my voice. Two months of it coming down to this woman, this fucking waitress at a fucking gentlemen's club, blackmailing me.

My free hand fists as I bring the tumbler to my lips once more, swallow the contents then stand.

"I need to go."

He stands too, puts his hand on my shoulder, eyes intent on me. "If you need me—"

"You'll be there?" I throw out before I can stop myself.

His jaw tightens. "Yes, I will, brother. And you fucking know it."

"Go home to your wife and kids, Jericho. You don't want to be involved in this."

I move away, but he steps in front of me. "I mean it, Zeke. I will be there. Anything you need. Whatever it is."

I study him. He does mean it, that much I can read on his face. But the truth is, the last three years living in Amsterdam with the excuse of expanding the family business, they've brought to the surface just how fresh the wounds of the past are. Just how raw the feeling of being abandoned by my older brother all those years ago when we all needed him most is. In a way, it's worse now than it was before, when Kimberly died, and Jericho was mourning her while in hiding with his little girl. Is it that I'm not happy for him to have found peace and a life with Isabelle? Am I so vile that I begrudge my brother his happiness when he, too, has suffered?

"Since you're offering, I'll hold on to Dex if you don't mind." Dex works for Jericho. I don't know how much he knows about the things Jericho has done or what I've done, but I know my brother trusts him. He's the driver who picked up Blue to bring her to work this evening.

That's not what he wanted to hear. It's clear on his face. He sighs. "Done."

I nod my thanks. "I need to go." I have preparations to make.

It takes him a moment to step out of the way, but he does.

I walk out of The Cat House and into the pouring rain. I don't bother with a coat, but let the rain drench me as I head toward my vehicle, the driver, opening the door of the backseat and apologizing for not having driven to meet me. Had he missed the call? I reassure him he's fine and give him the address to the old Bishop house. The property is adjacent to the St. James mansion, my one-time home, but I'll use the separate entrance. I lean back in my seat and watch the rain fall on this city I love. The city I miss. The one place I long to be but can never return to.

3

BLUE

I grip the edge of the counter, eyes closed while I wait for the dizziness to pass. Wait for the ringing in my ears to subside.

Everything is building on top of everything else. All the emails? It's a matter of time until my dad catches up with me and no matter what, I can't let him find Wren.

Now there's this on top of everything else. Ezekiel St. James depositing a dollar into my account and sending that middle finger emoji before showing up here, where I work. Granted it's a part of IVI, but he lives in Amsterdam. I know that. He shouldn't be here. I'd never have taken this job if there was any chance I'd run into him.

I know and you're fucked. That's the message he's sending. And I am well and truly fucked if I don't come up with something fast.

I bend down to splash cold water on my face. When I meet my reflection in the mirror, I see how red my eyes are, how dark the shadows beneath. I try to rub away the black eyeliner that smeared as I puked up the pasta I scarfed down before my shift. My stomach is in knots, and when I hold up my hands, they're shaking.

His silence in the beginning, when he first would have received my message, that was him taking his time until he figured out who I was. A man like him isn't just going to hand over a-hundred-grand when threatened with exposure. I overshot this, choosing him. I should never have targeted a man like him. He's powerful. I knew that, didn't I? All of the men who frequent this private club, who are members of The Society, you don't fuck with them.

But I wasn't exactly flush with options.

Shit. Shit. Shit.

Someone bangs on the locker room door once before pushing it open hard, the impact of the door against the wall making me jump even as I expected it.

Craven stands there looking furious and something else. Satisfied.

"You're on the clock, Blue."

I take a breath in, shift gears. Craven I can deal with. He's the kind of man I'm used to dealing with.

"I just puked. I don't think those men out there want me puking on them, do you?"

He was crossing the room toward me but pauses. I would laugh at his apparent fear of the word puke, but I can't.

"I must have had bad shrimp for dinner," I lie. I lay one hand on my stomach and cover my mouth with the other as if another wave is coming.

"For fuck's sake, that's disgusting," he says, turning away.

"It passed. It's okay." I take a deep breath. "I'll just brush my teeth and get back out there."

"No, that's fine." He hasn't moved closer and is regarding me differently than usual. Not leering. If only I'd known he was so squeamish from day one. "Go home. I'm not cleaning up puke."

"I'm just glad I didn't hurl all over Mr. St. James," I say, feeling a chill when I say his name out loud.

"Christ. Like I needed to deal with that." He shakes his head.

"Which one was he anyway?" I ask before I can stop myself.

"Both. They're brothers. Jericho and Ezekiel. They don't come in here often. I guess they won't be back since your little incident."

"Brothers?" I knew he had a brother but didn't know they hung out together.

He nods. "They left. I sure hope they're not going to file a complaint."

"They're both gone?"

"Yeah." He turns toward the door but stops before he walks out. "Get out of here. If it wasn't the shrimp and you have some bug, I don't want you infecting the other girls."

"Thanks for your concern." Asshole.

"You can make up your time this weekend," he says as he walks out the door.

I flip him off. Well, I flip off the door as it closes behind him. I won't be back this weekend. Or ever. Tonight's incident changes things. My plan was Canada but without that money, it's not happening. I can't take

Wren. If it were just me, I wouldn't care, I can sleep on the street. But Wren can't fend for herself. Not after what happened, how she is now. Canada was going to be more permanent. I can't just keep moving her. She won't understand and she needs stability. Some sense of security and safety. The facility she's at now, Oakwood Care Center, it's a decent place and Rudy is great with her.

Does she remember or even understand what's happened anymore? Or has her brain shut that part of her life off? Has it erased the memories? God. I fucking hope so.

I rinse my mouth once more and pull my hair out of the tight bun. I rub my scalp and ruffle my hair. I cut it shorter, so it just brushes my shoulders. I turn my face a little, touch the scar that's still somehow visible beneath the thick layer of foundation. I finger-comb my hair toward my face a little. It's not for the sake of vanity. I'm not vain. I just don't like looking at it. So, I turn away, slip off my heels and scoop them up on my way to my locker. I pull my sweatpants back on and put on my raincoat, then step into my sneakers. Grabbing my bag, I walk out of the changing room and toward the glass doors where I watch rain coming down in sheets. I guess I can't ask Craven for another ride, so I push the door open and hurry out meaning to run to the bus stop across the street. But before I'm even a few steps away, the Rolls Royce pulls up. The same chauffeur climbs out of the driver's side and hurries to open the back door for me.

"Oh, thank you!" I say gratefully. Maybe Craven has a tiny bit of humanity in him after all. He has nothing to gain by having me driven home, that's for sure.

I get in, my feet wet in my ratty shoes, my hair soaked and sticking to my head. I push it back from my face as the driver pulls out.

"God, I'm drenched. Thanks again," I say, but get no answer which isn't unusual. I notice the men of The Society, even staff in most cases, don't talk to us women. We're not quite first-class citizens here.

I push my hand into my bag and rifle through it to get my phone. Maybe I'm wrong. Maybe Ezekiel St. James had just made a mistake and has actually made the deposit and I'm just being paranoid. That could be it, couldn't it? I covered my tracks.

My bag is overfull of junk mostly, and as I rummage, I notice the driver take a left where he should take a right.

"You should go right there. It's faster. Just take the next turn. The roads connect," I say.

He glances into the rear-view mirror and it's the same man, I'm sure, but he doesn't give any indication he's even heard me. Well, I guess he gives one. A divider tinted a smokey black begins to go up from a pocket behind the front seats.

I watch it, confused, my mind slow to catch up as my body begins to pump blood faster, sending adrenaline through my veins, sounding an alarm I'm too slow to hear.

Danger.

Second time tonight I feel that word in my bones.

"What are you doing?" My arm shoots out, fingers curling around the glass to stop it rising. It's almost to the roof of the car and it doesn't stop neither does the man answer. I pull my fingers back, grabbing for the door handle, pulling and pulling, knowing it will be locked. Some stupid part of my brain that hasn't quite caught up tries to tell me it's just because we're in Drive. The locks always engage. It's a safety feature.

"Shit." I dump my bag out on the seat, my hands shaking hard. Half its contents spill onto the floor. My wallet, lipstick, powder, pens, gum, a half-eaten granola bar. Shit. The driver takes a turn and I look out the window but recognize nothing. Nothing except the lights of the city fading as we drive out onto quieter roads. Where houses are bigger. Where twelve-foot stone walls with tall iron gates cut them off from the rest of the world.

Where is it? Where the fuck is my phone?

I undo my seatbelt, listen to the *ding ding ding* alerting the driver as I drop down to the floor of the Rolls Royce to search for my phone. It's not here. It's gone. But who would I call anyway? Who could I call?

I climb back up to my seat, gather up my things and watch as we drive farther and farther away from any lights. I shiver not from cold but fear, loading my things back into my purse like that matters. Like anything matters. He's going to kill me. Ezekiel St. James is going to murder me. It's not like it's his first time. He's done it before. And that was his own father.

The car finally slows as we approach the open gates of a house set so far back from the road, I can just make out the light in a distant window. One light in a house that is so big, it can swallow up the apartment building I live in three times over and have room for dessert.

From what I can see, the grounds are meticulously

maintained and vast and I don't need to glance back to know that the gates behind me have sealed shut.

I fucked up this time. Well and truly fucked up.

The car comes to a stop at the stairs that lead to the front doors of the house. House. No, not a house. It's a fucking estate. The driver kills the engine, climbs out and he opens my door. Just opens it and stands there like he had earlier. Still formal in his uniform although the black leather gloves he's wearing give off a menacing vibe now.

"Miss," he says when I don't move.

I'm going to be sick again. I would be if there was anything left in my stomach. I think about the pot in the sink of my shitty apartment. The lone fork.

"Wh..." I clear my throat because I'm struggling to form words. "Where am I?"

"Miss." He gestures for me to climb out.

I do. Because what else am I going to do? I'm sure he'd have no qualms about dragging me out of the vehicle and into that house.

But if Ezekiel St. James was going to kill me or have me killed, he wouldn't bring me to his house. DNA. He'd be better off having me run down when I cross a street or something. It'd be easier and less mess for him to clean up. He needs something from me, at least before he kills me.

That's what I tell myself as I walk in the direction the chauffeur points and enter the vast, cold house. From the little bit of light in the hallway, I see all the furniture is covered with dust cloths. Maybe he had that done since he's living in Amsterdam now. If this is his house, it would sit empty I guess while he's away. What do people as rich as Ezekiel St. James do when they go away? It's not like he's going to list it on Airbnb or something.

I keep glancing behind me at the driver who still has the collar of his coat turned up, his hat drawn down low on his forehead, those gloves on his big hands.

"Where are we going?" I hear myself ask. I know he won't answer.

He just tilts his head toward the stairs, and I begin climbing and once I'm on the second-floor landing, I walk down the dark corridor toward the last door, the only door that is ajar, a dim lamp burning inside. I stop just outside of it, every hair on my body standing on end, every instinct on full alert, in panic mode. I'm not sure how I'm keeping it together, actually. Like a duck, on the surface I may look calm but just beneath, I'm paddling like crazy to stay afloat.

"In," he says.

I look over my shoulder at him. The man is a giant. A solid beast I know I can't outrun let alone get past. So, I enter the room and before I can even turn around, he's closed the door and I hear a lock engaging.

A lock on the outside. Of course.

I turn to my surroundings again, a small, sparse room. It's not a basement though, right? That's something? There's carpet here. If he was going to kill me, he wouldn't do it where there's a carpet.

It's a corner room with three windows. Decorative drapes stand open on each. I glance out of one window and regret it instantly when I see the garden's atmospheric lighting, the vast area beyond dense with trees. That stone wall.

My purse slips from my hand, and I slide my jacket off with it. I'm freezing and sweating at once. I turn my back to the outside and grip the windowsill, squeezing my eyes shut and telling myself to breathe. I wrap my arms around myself and force my eyes open, make myself take it all in, to figure out an exit. An out. Some strategy for when he comes for me. Because he will come, Ezekiel St. James. He'll want to know how I found out. Where I got my information. If anyone else knows.

And then what? What will he do? Let me walk away? I don't think so.

Wren.

Does he know about Wren?

Would he hurt her?

Before I can go into a full blow panic, I make my leaden legs move, taking in the sparse furnishings. An armchair. An ottoman. A table and a chair against the wall. That single lamp on top of it. It has a glass base.

I go to it, pick it up. Hold it in two hands. I'd prefer a heavier base, something I can get my hands around and swing. But this, the glass, it's something. I set it down for now and head to the door that ends up leading to an empty closet. Another one opens into a bathroom. I switch on the light. Only one bulb over the vanity works but it's enough to show off the marble in the small room, the shower, no bathtub in here. A lone pedestal sink and no cabinets to search. There's an empty towel rack and an old-fashioned looking toilet, one of those with the bowl high up and a long chain to flush.

I switch on the tap and it hiccups before water spurts out, then begins to pour ice cold. I guess no one has used this bathroom in a while. I cup my hands and drink some then switch it off, wipe my hands on my sweats since there's no towel. My hair is drying. It's no longer stuck to my head. There's no cleaning up the smeared eyeliner. I look like I've been through it, and *it* hasn't even begun yet.

I walk back to the outer room and try the door. Still locked, as expected. Still silent beyond it, too. I look back at the lamp. It's my only option. Switching the bathroom light back on so I'm not left in complete darkness, I unplug it, carry it into the bathroom. I close the door behind me and, without overthinking it, I hit the base against the sink hard enough to crack it. The glass is strong, that's good. I do it again, careful not to shatter it, cringing at the sound, hoping if the driver or St. James are in the hallway, they don't hear it.

This time, the glass breaks into multiple large shards. I bend to pick up the best one, test the edge. Like a knife. Good.

I walk back out into the bedroom carefully carrying the lamp. I'd rather leave it off but it's too dark and I can't see anything without it, so I plug it back in, turning the part of the base that's not completely destroyed toward the room for when he comes for me.

My purse and coat are on the floor. I dig out some tissues from inside my bag and wrap them around one side of the glass, so I don't cut myself when I cut him. I guess he had someone look through my stuff and take my cell phone while I was working.

I stand, look at my makeshift dagger, a shiv, I guess. I feel calmer for it. Carefully tucking it into the pocket of my oversized sweats, I walk to the door. I need to get out of here. I need to figure out some plan for Wren and me. I can't just sit here and wait for him.

"Hey!" I call out. "Hey! Let me out of here!" I slap my hands against the door. It's loud and it hurts my palms, but I do it again. I want this over with. I need it over with. I need him to come. This was a mistake. Blackmailing a man like Ezekiel St. James was a huge mistake.

There's nothing though. No response. He doesn't come. I'm not even sure the driver is outside my door or in the house at all. Hell, maybe he's just going to leave me here to starve to death.

I pace the room, try the windows, but they're sealed tight. Not sure what I'd do if I could open one anyway, scale the wall? Not likely. I'm not Spiderman.

Again, I go to the door and bang and holler. Again, nothing. The image of the brothers at The Cat House comes to mind. How they'd looked in their cloaks and masks. How big they were when they stood. How strong the one who wrapped his hands around my arms just a little tighter than necessary in the guise of helping me when I would have fallen.

Tears threaten but I wipe the few that escape away and tell myself to stop it. It's pathetic and I'm scared, yes, but I need to think about Wren. What will happen to her if I don't get out of here?

"Let me out!" I scream again, the words ending on a sob as I slam my fists into the door and this time, this time, there is something. Someone slams their fist into it from the other side and I jump backward, my heart hammering. I think it was better when there was no response.

It happens again, that fist slamming so hard the door rattles in its hinges, and I back up, wondering how long someone has been out there. Wondering if he was just listening. Waiting. Getting in my head.

The lock disengages and I hurry away from the door, my heart in my throat. I slide my hand into my pocket and close it around the shiv, wincing when it slices my palm because those few tissues wrapped around it don't offer much protection.

I back up as the door opens. Light from the hallway illuminates his dark form, making him appear bigger. Darker. More menacing as he stands in his cloak and mask and I swear he's taller and bigger than he was at the club, eyes on fire with power, and fury, knowing his dominion over me. I hear the pathetic sound my throat makes. I'm sure he hears it too.

There's a part of me that wishes it was the driver. It's not. It's Ezekiel St. James. He steps inside and he doesn't stop until he eats up the space between us and backs me into the wall. He towers over me and the sight of him in that cloak and mask is fucking terrifying. I've never been this scared in my life. Not even the night that changed my life forever. The night that sent us on the run.

The sheer size of him, his presence larger than life, his fury a palpable thing in the room with us, it's all too much. It's all too fucking much.

4

EZEKIEL

Terror has her muttering senseless words. Has her frozen to the spot, her back pressed to the wall. Her narrow shoulders shake hard. She brings a hand to my chest, her fingers trembling. It's as if she's checking to make sure I'm real. Her touch is so very insignificant, like a butterfly landing on a lion. Her eyes search my face behind the mask. She is unable to hold my gaze.

I could end her. Here. Now. No one would know. All it would take would be a quick twisting of her tiny little neck. The slamming of her head against the wall. Just one of my hands pressing against her throat to squeeze the breath from her. To steal the life from her. She's that much smaller than me. Maybe five-feet-two-inches and petite. Physically, she doesn't stand a chance.

And yet she dares to try and extort money from me. To threaten to expose me. To threaten Zoë and Jericho and all those about whom I care.

She makes a sound, something like a broken little bird caught in the jaws of a predator.

Broken. No. That's not right. Not with this girl. It's something else. She's a fighter. A survivor. That sound is the sound of someone who is caught. Who is desperate.

And that makes her dangerous.

In the next instant, I realize just how dangerous when, out of nowhere, she's got a fucking knife to my throat.

"Get away from me. Get the fuck away from me!"

The blade cuts, sharp and burning. A warm drop of blood slides down my neck. But it's a shallow cut.

"Blue," I say, low and slow. She's not going to do it. She'd have sliced an artery if she was going to do it. If I'm wrong, well, there'll be no turning back, but I have a gut feeling. Fighter or not, she's not a killer.

"I said get the fuck away from me, asshole!"

I shoot my arm out and grip her wrist. She gasps at the speed of the movement. I twist until she yelps and spin her around, drawing her to me with one arm around her middle the other a vise around her wrist.

Where the fuck did she get a knife? I had her bag and coat pockets searched.

"You're going to make a mess on the carpet," I say, my voice a deep timbre vibrating against her ear. She shudders and her fear, the smell of it, the presence of it, it stirs that darkness inside me that lies dormant, but there. Always there. "Drop it," I tell her.

"Fuck you." She rams the elbow of her free arm into my stomach. A fighter. Like I thought. But no match for me.

"That wasn't very nice, Blue." I grip her free arm, whirl her around, slam her back into the wall.

She grunts, her head bouncing off, and drops the knife. She's disoriented. I watch her blink, give her a minute for her eyes to slowly refocus on my face. They're pretty. A deep, cerulean blue several shades lighter than her hair. And as her pupils refocus, they grow dark with fury. Not fear. Or maybe that's there too, beneath the fury.

"You're going to stop fighting me now, Blue. And you're going to get on your knees and put your hands behind your head. You hear me?"

"Go fuck yourself, asshole."

One corner of my mouth curves upward. I didn't think I'd enjoy this as much as I am.

I loosen my hold on her wrists. I'll let her run. Give chase. I can outrun her. Overpower her. Those things aren't an issue. She can't weigh more than a-hundred-and-ten-pounds soaking wet. I'll let her wear herself out because this one is not going down easy.

But when she tugs her arms free, she doesn't run or try to get away from me, like I expect. She grips my arms instead and attempts to knee me in the groin. I catch her leg between my thighs and let her have her little fight. Let her think she has some control in this.

She doesn't.

She wrestles, tries to scoot past me this way and that. She gets to the door and out into the hallway. She's almost to the stairs when I catch up with her, tugging her backward against my chest by her hair.

"Blue." I shift my grip to her arms and lean down toward her ear. Before I can say anything, though, she drops her head then slams it backward. I turn my face just in time, so she hits my jaw and not my nose. That would have hurt.

I growl, irritated.

"That wasn't very nice."

I lift her over my shoulder. She's light as a feather. She yelps. I smack her ass and she pounds against my back as I walk her back into the small bedroom. I drop her on her ass and wait for her to scramble up to her feet before gripping her wrist with one hand and a handful of hair with the other to force her to her knees.

"I told you to kneel."

Her free hand wraps around the arm that has a fistful of her hair as I crouch down while bringing her to her knees. Once she's down, I grin.

"You'd better learn to do as I say," I tell her calmly.

"Asshole!" She shoots out her arm and snatches away my mask, clawing flesh as she does it. Only when that's done does she stop. Does she draw back, that mask in her hand, her breathing ragged, as ragged as mine.

"Finished?" I ask, jerking her head back.

She cries out, drops the mask. I kick away the knife and as soon as I release her, she falls forward onto her hands, panting.

I give her a minute to catch her breath while I walk the few steps to where the knife is. But it's not a knife at all. It's a thick shard of glass with blood on its edges. Mine. Hers too, when I glance at her to find her holding the wrist of the hand which is pouring blood onto the white carpet.

"Where did you learn this trick? Prison?"

"I've never been to prison, asshole."

"I'm done hearing myself referred to as asshole."

"You prefer ass wipe?"

I toss the glass far enough away she won't get to it and walk back to her. There, I crouch down again and am glad to see her cringe back. At least until she catches herself doing it.

"What was that?" I ask, my face inches from hers. "Didn't quite catch it."

She glares, but keeps her mouth shut. Good girl.

"What's your name?" I ask.

"Blue Masterson."

"Your real name."

She doesn't answer my question. "I'm bleeding here. I need stitches. There could be glass in the cut."

"That'd be too bad for you but too good for me. Name."

"Blue. Blue Masterson," she says more loudly.

I exhale, shake my head. "If you think you know what I did," I start, referencing her first message to me. "Don't you think you should watch yourself around me, *Blue*?"

At that her expression changes. She searches my face. I wonder what she sees. What I see, even in this dimly lit room, is that she's young. Nowhere near the twenty-seven on her ID. She's completely out of her league. And the look in her eyes in that moment, the uncertainty, the expression of someone lost, it triggers something inside me. Because I know this look. I've seen it before.

And I've ignored it.

I shake my head. Now is not the time to reminisce. I need to remember why she's here. Why I was forced to return to this place that holds all the bad memories of my past.

What I know about Blue Masterson isn't much. But she somehow got her hands on information about me that, if it gets out, will hurt those I care about and possibly destroy me. That's not nothing. She's not some pickpocket, dollar store thief. She is much more capable than that. And I need to know exactly what she knows and how she came to know it before I can make any decisions about her well-being. Her future. Whether or not she'll have one.

"How old are you?"

"Twenty-seven."

"And I'm Santa Clause."

Her face says it all. Cocky arrogance replaces what I saw an instant ago. She clenches her jaw tight, lips in a sneer, head tilted so she's somehow managing to look down her nose at me from her position kneeling at my feet.

"How. Old. Are. You?"

"Twenty. Seven." She mimics my tone.

I smile. She smiles wider.

"Cute," I say, and she dips her head like she's taking a fucking bow and before she even sees me move, I fist that handful of hair again. This time, she lets out a scream as I draw her up by her hair. It's painful, I'm sure. She mewls, her neck twisted as she clutches my forearm with both hands. I march her toward the desk, lift the chair to set it out of the way and push her face-down over the desk. I kick her legs out wide to stand between them, grip the waistband of the oversized sweatpants and tug them off.

She gasps but I'm not done yet. I flip the skirt of the uniform, if you can call it that, up over her ass and smack a cheek hard.

She clenches, gasps, her back stiffening.

I hook a finger into the snaps at the crotch and with one tug, they snap open, and her ass is right there on display just for me. I take a minute to enjoy the sight of her sweet, round cheeks, the skin just beginning to pink.

But only good girls get spankings.

And Blue here is not a good girl.

I cup her sex, dig my fingers into tender flesh.

"No!" She begins her fight anew, adrenaline must be coursing through her veins. She flails her arms, pushing back from the desk, and I shift my grip to take her wrists. I draw them out, and lean over her, pinning her with my weight, reminding myself she's not here to be fucked.

"I asked you a question," I say, voice low and deep and somehow calm sounding.

"Nineteen! I'm fucking Nineteen!"

"You sure?"

She nods, rattling off her birthday as if to prove she's not lying. "Please don't hurt me!"

"Please don't hurt you?" I ask with a laugh. I'm sure she can feel my erection between her ass cheeks. She's very still as I straighten, bringing both wrists to her lower back and shifting them into one of my hands. I spank her again, harder and she yelps. I look down at the sight of my handprint forming on the soft, smooth flesh. "Why do you think we're here, Blue Masterson?" I ask, gripping a cheek and drawing it out, taking in the pink slit of her pussy, the tight ring of her asshole.

"Please." It's a quiet plea.

"What's the matter? No please *asshole*?" I shift my gaze down as I say the words and she stiffens when she feels my thumb against that very orifice.

"Oh God. Please don't."

I press the pads of those fingers against the warm, tight hole and lean over her again. "Do you know I could finish you right here, right now, dump your body, your shitty bag and coat. It'd be like you never existed at all." I rub her asshole. "Of course, I'd take what I wanted first. What is owed to me, considering your attempt at blackmail and extortion."

"I'm sorry. I just…"

"And you know what? No one would even give a shit. No one would miss you, would they, *Blue*?"

"I just…" She turns her head to the side, attempts to wipe her eyes and nose on her shoulder.

"No wait," I continue, straightening, releasing her wrists and gripping the far edge of the desk, my hands on either side of her face. Because she lost the right to a defense the day she decided to send that first email.

She looks at my hands, big and strong, oh the damage they can do. I wait for her to shift her gaze up to me before I finish my sentence.

"Wait. Someone *would* miss you," I say.

Her expression changes wholly then, all the fire and fury, gone. Tears drop from her blue eyes. She's prettier for it. It's a weird thought I know. A sick one maybe. But I know the stock I come from.

"I'll repeat myself once more, Blue," I say, drawing

back to give her space to do as I command. "Get on your knees."

I should question her and be done with her. Finish her. That's all. But there is that command and something inside me twists and stretches and yawns to life. Something dark and ruthless and feral as a starved beast in the wild.

She straightens, wiping her eyes and nose with the inside of her wrist. And she drops to her knees. Because I have her.

5

BLUE

"That's better."

His voice is a dark vibration that makes me shiver.

He knows. He knows about Wren. How did I ever think I could get away with this? With a man like him?

"Where do your hands go?" he asks in that low, deceptively controlled tone.

I don't realize I've got my left hand over my right to staunch the bleeding. The cut is deeper than I thought. The one on his neck has already closed. I did more damage to myself than him with my homemade weapon.

"Blue," he draws out my name, the sound of it menacing on his tongue. This is a powerful man. A dangerous one. What the fuck was I thinking? The others, there were two, they were different, photos of them cheating on their wives. They paid and it was done. This is something else entirely.

I raise my hands and set them at the back of my head. Blood trails down the inside of my arm. I follow his gaze down and see how the bodysuit with its snaps undone, which is already too small and tight, leaves me wholly exposed below my waist. I bring my thighs together.

He slowly drags his gaze to mine. There's a small, upward curve to his lips that makes something in my stomach flutter. He had his hands on me. The most intimate parts of my body.

He crouches down so we're almost at eye level.

"Please don't hurt her. She had nothing to do with this. She doesn't know anything."

"She?"

I blink. Was he guessing? Was it a stupid guess and I just gave it away?

His eyes search my face and I take in their silvery-grey shade, the coldness of them. I find I can't look at them for too long and shift my gaze to study his face, the five o'clock shadow along his jaw, the sharp line of it, the hardness of his mouth. I wonder how he'd look smiling. Handsome, I think. Not kind though. There is nothing kind about this man.

When he reaches out a hand to brush the hair back from my face, I flinch with the contact of skin. He pauses, holds up a finger, raises his eyebrows. His silent instruction for me to be still. His thumb brushes my jaw before his fingers curl around it and gently, which is absurd that I'd think anything this man does to me is gentle, he tilts my face a little so he can get a better look. I'm sure my makeup has worn off. The ugly, still-angry pink scar that spans my cheek is visible. The Frankenstein-like marks my clumsy stitching left.

His eyes narrow. I tug free of his grasp and give a

shake of my head, so my hair falls across my left cheek to hide it at least a little.

He meets my gaze, and I find myself staring into those wolfish eyes again. I can't read him. But he's trying to read me. He's curious about the scar or the stitching, probably. Anyone who sees it stares. That's why I wear such heavy makeup. Well, that and so my dad doesn't find me. He has friends on the street keeping an eye out for a woman with a hideous scar across her face. Think Bride of Frankenstein.

I'm trying to come up with a smart answer for when he asks but he surprises me when, instead of asking, he reaches for my hand, the one that's throbbing, still bleeding.

I hold it out for him to see.

He takes it, brings it between us and turns it this way and that to look at the cut, then meets my gaze with a grin on his face.

"We'll need to stitch that up. It's not going to close on its own."

I nod but stop. Him mentioning stitches is the last thing I expect because what's he going to do, take me to the ER? I doubt it.

"I need to go to the hospital."

He raises his eyebrows. "Oh, I don't think so."

"But—"

"I'll do my best. Use all my best sewing skills." My mouth drops open. "Spoiler, I'm not very good." He winks as he straightens to his full height, which is well over six feet. I'm only five-feet-two-inches and kneeling before him, well, it's intimidating.

He grins as if reading my mind.

"You're not sewing me up," I say.

"I can't let you bleed to death, can I?"

I shudder at the way he says it. "What are you going to do to me?"

He holds out his hand, palm up. "I just told you. I'm going to sew that closed. Get up, Blue."

"I mean... After."

He shrugs a shoulder. "We'll talk and what I do next, well, that'll depend on you. Up. I don't want you bleeding out."

I follow his gaze to my hand. I don't think I'll bleed out, but it doesn't look like it'll close on its own. I don't take his hand but stand on my own, using the table for balance. It takes a minute for the dizziness to pass once I'm up. The ringing starts. I close my eyes, draw a deep breath in, then slowly exhale.

I need to keep it together. For Wren. He hasn't killed me yet. He hasn't hurt me, not really. The damage to my hand is self-inflicted.

"Blue, you with me?"

I open my eyes, nod. I eye my sweats on the floor and when I bend to pick them up, he lets me. I pull them on, wincing at the pain in my hand, not bothering with the stupid snaps of the uniform that rode up my crotch anyway.

He gestures for the door, and I take a clumsy step. He catches my arm.

"What's wrong with you?" he asks.

I swallow, my neck craned to look at him because the top of my head barely comes to his chin.

I try to tug free. "I'm fine."

"Hm." He keeps hold of my arm as we walk out of the small room, into the hallway and down the stairs. I take in the dimly lit rooms and all those dust cloths as we make our way into the kitchen. It's a large, open space with checkered black and white tiles set in a harlequin pattern. A stone island is central with four stools on one side, a stovetop and sink on the other. The driver who brought me here is sitting on one of those stools and from the smell of it, drinking freshly brewed coffee. He's reading a paper he puts down when he sees us and raises his eyebrows at my captor.

"Dex, if you can head over to the Oakwood Care Cent—"

"Wait, what?" I cut in, panicked. I step in front of Ezekiel and set my free hand on his chest, not missing how firm and muscled it is. "We're talking. You said—"

"Incentive for you to tell the truth."

"She doesn't know about any of this. I swear. I swear on my life!"

"Relax, Blue."

"She won't understand! She's not part of this. She's not—"

"I said relax." He takes my elbows and gives them a warning squeeze. "Dex is going to wait in his car in the parking lot. He won't enter unless he gets a call from me. You understand?"

"Just leave her out of it. All of it. I'll tell you what you want to know. I promise."

"Sadly, your promises don't carry much weight here."

He gestures to Dex who is already folding up his paper. "Go. I'll be in touch."

Dex nods and is gone. I try to pull free of Ezekiel to do what I don't know but his grip hardens as he walks me toward the sink.

"Hey," he says, forcing me to look at him. "I said relax. You tell me what I want to know, and she'll be fine."

I don't miss the fact that he says, 'she'll be fine' not 'you'll both be fine.'

"But if you give me a hard time—"

"I won't."

"I'm glad to hear that. Just a few things to cover before we begin. You and I are alone in this house. The door is locked. The property is vast and surrounded by a twelve-foot stone wall. The gate is closed. Just so we're all on the same page here. Do not make me chase you. Understand?"

I nod.

"Good."

He turns me toward the sink and switches on the tap, setting my hand under it. I wince and try to pull away, but he holds it beneath the flow.

"Keep it here. Understand?"

I nod. He lets go and I watch him take off his cloak and drape it over the back of a stool at the counter. He then begins to rifle through several cabinets. A few moments later, he finds what he needs. I turn to see him taking a large first-aid kit out of a cabinet before bending down for something else.

"There won't be anything in that thing to sew me up,"

I say. "You need to take me to the ER." And from there, I can take off.

"You're right about the first part," he says, straightening and pulling out a second, smaller box that I recognize. That makes me queasy. "No idea why Bishop would have had this, but I'll call it your lucky day," he says, coming toward me. He nudges me out of the way and scrubs his hands before switching off the water.

I don't know who Bishop is but that's not my concern right now.

"It's fine, you actually don't need to sew me up," I say, eyes on the kit as he goes through it. "It's better already. It's fine."

He looks at my hand, which is not fine, takes out one of the gauze bandages and wraps it around the cut. "I'm not going to lie. It's going to hurt."

"And let me guess, you're going to enjoy it." I hold onto the gauze as he carries both boxes toward the table and sets them down. I notice the bottle of whiskey and the glass.

"Anesthesia," he says. "It's old fashioned but better than nothing. Sit."

"I'll do it myself," I say, sitting down. My hand is throbbing, and I feel lightheaded.

"I don't think so." He takes the seat across from mine, pours a generous serving of whiskey into the glass and pushes it toward me.

"Drink that."

"I'm fine."

"Suit yourself." He draws his chair closer and takes my hand, gently peeling the gauze from it.

"I really think it'll be okay without stitches," I say, my voice higher as the reality that he will actually sew me up hits.

He puts on the gloves included in the pack, unpacks a disinfecting pad, and gently touches it to the skin around the cut. I wince, sucking in a breath, and, keeping his head bent over his work, he lifts his gaze to mine.

"Drink the whiskey, Blue."

I shake my head, my breathing shallow, my heart racing. "Just do it. Hurry." Because I know it's not going to close on its own and I just need to get through this. I grip the edge of my chair with my free hand and watch him take one of the hooked needles out of its package. "Oh God."

"Afraid of needles?"

"I'm afraid of you with those needles."

He smiles and it's the first genuine smile I've seen. It somehow calms me and when he sets my hand on his thigh, I feel a strange sensation deep in my stomach. The movement is intimate. Tender almost.

"Like I said, this will hurt," he tells me, that same smile morphing into something else, making me shake my head at the direction my thoughts just took.

My eyes are locked on the needle. He's right about it hurting. It's going to hurt like fucking hell.

I am sure he doesn't trust that I won't pull away instinctively and closes one hand over my wrist. He holds that hand in place as he brings the needle with its suturing thread toward the wound.

"Isn't there glue or something in there?" I ask

panicked, tugging at my hand but unable to pull it out of his grasp.

"Sorry, no," he says not sounding remotely sorry. He doesn't bother to look up, and, before I can open my mouth to ask if he's sure, the needle is in.

I bite my lip so hard I taste blood. Tears sting my eyes, and I can't help the sound I make when he draws it out of the inside of the wound.

He glances up at me. Grins. "Drink the whiskey."

I shake my head, trying to stop crying. "Please hurry."

He gets back to work, and I whimper as he draws the needle out of the other side.

"You have to tie it off first. Then do the next one. You have to tie them off—"

"Shh." He begins doing just that and I'm not sure if it's because he's watched a video or practiced or what, but he is neat and precise, and he's done with the first stitch sooner than I expect.

"How did you know to do that?" I ask. When I sewed up my face, I was nowhere near as precise nor was I remotely calm. But in my defense, my hands wouldn't stop shaking and all I had to go on was watching my sister practice on orange peels and a YouTube video on suturing a wound.

He shrugs a shoulder and gestures to the whiskey.

This time, I don't refuse it because it hurts like hell. So, I drink down the entire glass, swallow it like it's water even as it burns my throat, and when I'm done, I pour myself a little more and drink that too.

"Good girl," he says and pushes the needle into my skin again for a second stitch. Nausea has me squeezing my eyes shut. "Did you do your face yourself?" he asks casually.

I nod. "Yes," I hear myself answer.

"You're not very good," he says, almost making me laugh as he draws the needle out of the other end and what would have been a laugh turns into a sad little whimper.

"It hurts. It really hurts."

"I imagine it does." He looks up from my hand to my face. "Are you going to pass out?"

I'm sure I look white as a ghost, but I shake my head. I have to think of Wren now. I have to convince this man that I am not a threat to him. Convince him to let me go. And him doing this now, it's something. He could just let me bleed out, but he's not.

"What's your name? Your real name?" he asks, starting on the third stitch. By my calculation, I'll need at least six, but I have a feeling he can double that count if he wants to.

"Bluebird," I say.

He looks up, eyebrows high.

"My mom had a thing."

"Bluebird what?"

"Bluebird Smith." I rub the tip of my nose with my free arm, then wipe away the involuntary tears he's forcing.

"Bluebird Smith?" His eyebrows disappear into his hairline but I just nod. "Okay, Bluebird Smith. Tell me. What do you know about the events of the night my father's car went off a cliff?"

6

EZEKIEL

Bluebird Smith. I believe the Bluebird part. It's too odd a name to make up. But the last name is a lie.

I push the needle past the resistance of skin and hear her intake of breath. It hurts, I know. I couldn't lessen the pain if I wanted to and I'm not sure I want to.

"I need a break," she says.

I look at her. She's pale. I'd be surprised if she didn't need a break, actually.

"I'm going to be sick," she adds.

"Breathe." I wait, watch her as she does as she's told. I'm surprised by her naiveté. Her trust, almost. In me. It tells me a few things. She's not the experienced criminal I expected my blackmailer to be. And she's in way over her head.

"Better?" I ask and she nods. "Good. Now answer my question."

"I... Not much," she says. I wait. Tug a little at the stitch making her wince. It's mean but she has only herself to blame for her predicament and I don't just mean the cut. "I know your brother, Jericho, has seen video footage of you coming and then leaving a hotel in Austria on the night of the accident." I still don't continue because how the hell does she know that? "He had been in touch with the manager about it. And your name isn't anywhere on the hotel guest list on any night in that whole week. That's all. That's all I know."

"That's all? So, you decided to blackmail me for being in a hotel in Austria?"

"You took the bait, didn't you? What does that say?"

No way that's all. I shift my gaze back to her hand to close off that stitch, tugging at the skin a little as I make the knot. She winces.

"Keep talking," I tell her.

She reaches for the whiskey, but I push it away. "You've had enough."

"Why do you care?"

"I don't. I just don't want you passing out before I get my answers. Ready?"

She swallows, nods.

I look at her again after pushing the needle in for stitch number four. "Keep talking, Blue."

"I know your brother paid the hotel manager a chunk of cash to get rid of the footage, but he didn't."

Jericho had paid him to have those files erased. That much I know. "And he got hold of you and wanted to know if you wanted to buy a video of me coming and going from a hotel? Sounds logical," I say.

"He suspected you of tampering with the car. He said as much. You threw away a duffel bag he picked up."

Ah.

She pauses because I must give something away. It was stupid on my part to throw that duffel away at the hotel.

"Why else would you have been there at that hotel in disguise?" she asks, eyes intent on me, a note of confidence to her tone.

"I'd hardly say I was disguised."

"You didn't even use your name."

"Maybe I was meeting a lover."

Her cheeks flush pink momentarily. It's not a reaction I expect from a woman blackmailing me for a-hundred-grand. I make a mental note and bend my head to continue to the next suture.

"You lied," she says.

I glance up at her, raising my eyebrows.

"The stitches. You've done this before."

"I thought I wanted to be a surgeon once upon a time. Even went to medical school for a year before my father decided I needed to work for the family business. But we're not talking about me. Tell me what else you have that led you to believe I would deposit a-hundred-thousand-dollars into a random, anonymous account?"

"You didn't fly to Austria, not commercially, anyway. Everything was a secret," she says.

"How do you know that?"

She scratches the tip of her nose, shrugs the shoulder of her free arm. "It's not that hard to get into people's computers if you know what you're doing."

"And you know what you're doing?"

"I'm learning. Did little things like hacking into my

high-school's system to change a grade or two for a few friends."

"A convict from the start." The whiskey is working, loosening her tongue, relaxing her. To be fair, it's not only whiskey.

"It was just for fun. I was bored mostly."

"Okay so you found out about my visit to Austria from a man who wanted to make a buck selling information, saw that video footage from the hotel and decided I had something to do with my father's accident? That's a stretch, isn't it?"

"The bag, remember. I saw the contents of the duffel." She scratches her nose again and this time, I take notice of the casual act.

"Did you?" That could be a problem. "And where is the bag now?"

"I can't tell you that, can I? Not until I have that money and my sister, and I are out of New Orleans."

"Your sister who is in a facility that deals with brain injuries."

She nods, her forehead wrinkling with worry.

"Why do you want to get out of New Orleans so badly?"

"That's none of your business."

"I'd say anything I want to know is my business, considering the situation we find ourselves in." I get the feeling the alcohol, the little drug I slipped into her cup and me taking care of her wounded hand rather than wrapping mine around her pretty little neck have given her a warm, fuzzy feeling. A false sense of security. She's got the idea she's gained the upper hand and she's getting cocky, the little extortionist.

"Your brother paid a lot of money to the hotel manager to lose that video, but he should have taken better care to make sure it was deleted properly. It wasn't. That shitty guy is a mid-level manager of a shitty hotel. He's greedy and dishonest."

"Sounds like someone I'm getting to know."

"I'm neither of those things. There's a big difference between me and him. And there's more if you'd care to hear it."

"I'm all ears."

"That hotel manager recorded the conversation between your brother and himself."

"Did he?" I will kill the bastard myself if this is true. "Here's what I don't understand. How would this shitty mid-level manager, to use your words, think to reach out to you with all this? Why not try to blackmail me himself?"

She shrugs a shoulder, her eyelids drooping. "Maybe he didn't have the stomach for it."

"But you do?"

"Are you almost done?"

"How do you know him anyway?"

"Doesn't matter."

"It does to me."

"I don't feel very good." She says and I see how she sways a little before catching herself.

"No?"

"If something happens to me, the police will know."

"Is that so? What about your sister disappearing? What will that do?"

She opens her mouth, closes it. That furrow is back between her eyebrows.

"I think you're lying about that part at the very least, Little Convict. And I think you forget who you're dealing with." I pause. "Tell me. Who are you running from? Because you're running from someone."

She opens her mouth, surprised at my question. My guess. Her expression changes. The naïve girl of earlier is back. She rocks in her seat, her free arm hanging at her side, her head drooping. She's smaller than I realized, and my dosage is most likely off.

"Almost done. Don't pass out just yet," I say, leaning her back against the chair and bending my head to finish stitching her up while I think.

I left loose ends, and I'll need to tie those up. Blue or Bluebird or whatever her name is, she's not greedy or dishonest, at least I don't think so. She's on the run from someone she finds scarier than me. And she's worried about her sister. I may not have all the information yet, but there is one thing I know for sure and that is she's not walking out of here tonight. I put in three more stitches and by the time I'm done, I see how her shoulders have slumped. Her head bobs and her eyes have lost their focus.

"There," I say.

She looks down at her neatly stitched hand then shifts her gaze to me, her movements slow. She looks at the bottle of whiskey, then picks up the glass and peers at the remnants. She scrunches up her forehead. She's sort of cute with her chopped hair, the top layer of which is blue, the natural shade dark. It's a dye and cut done at home from the looks of it. But still, she's pretty enough it doesn't matter. Even with that scar on her face.

"Is that just whiskey?" she asks.

I smile. "Not used to it?" I take off the gloves.

She shakes her head, slow motion. "It's not that." She looks up at me, again cocking her head. "Is it?"

"Is it what?"

"Just..." Before she finishes, she slides sideways off the seat. I'm on my feet in an instant to scoop her up, careful to catch her injured hand and set it on her stomach.

"No, you little convict. It's not just whiskey. Don't you know the first rule when dealing with men like me? When threatening men like me?"

"What did you do?" She struggles, trying to get out of my arms as I carry her out of the kitchen, back down the hall and up the stairs to the bedroom I prepared for her.

"Don't drink anything your enemy offers you unless you've seen him drink it first."

"What did you... give me?" she croaks.

I draw the blanket back and lay her down. She struggles to keep her eyes from closing but she won't win. I sit on the edge of the bed, brush her hair back from her face as she tries to fight off sleep.

"What..."

"Just a little something to help you sleep while I find out exactly who the fuck you are."

7

EZEKIEL

She'll be out for the next twelve hours. Maybe more, given her size. The sleeping pills were mixed into the little bit of whiskey in the glass she drank from.

I look at her face as she sleeps. I say her name in my head, Bluebird Smith. I could pick up the sister. That would be the surest way to get to the truth. I don't know exactly what is wrong with her. All I know is that Oakwood Care Center specializes in brain injuries. But I'm curious about the little convict here.

I slip her well-worn sneakers off her feet. They're bare, her toenails a blue that matches her hair. I guess it's her favorite color. I drag the sweatpants off next. They're bloody from her cut, as are my slacks. She's not wearing underwear, as I already ascertained, and my gaze catches on the shaved slit of her pussy before I sit her up, leaning her against myself as I draw the bodysuit off over her head then lay her back down. I toss the scrap of a uniform onto the floor along with the rest of her things.

I take in her naked body. She's slender with full, round breasts, her nipples a deep pink. They tighten beneath my gaze as if I were touching her. I let my gaze trace a path over her flat stomach, to the slit of her sex. I'm hard at the sight of her like this. Not sure what that says about me, so I draw in a breath and return my gaze to her face, turning it to examine the scar. I push strands of blue and black hair off her cheek.

The scar is a four-inch-long jagged line. Not a knife, more like breaking glass with your face. It's not fresh but when I smear away more of the heavily applied foundation with my thumb, I see it's still pink. I imagine her looking in a mirror, hands shaking as she mustered up the courage to stitch herself up. I have to give it to her. It takes balls. Which confirms to me that she's desperate. I have no doubt she's running and the money she tried to extort from me her last resort.

There's some part of me that softens knowing that she's running from whoever did this to her. Hurt her.

I trace the scar, feel the hard tissue that's formed beneath, trace the five stitch marks, which are widely spaced and crooked. It will be visible for the rest of her life.

I have wondered for years now if it is somehow easier to bear the scars on the outside rather than the inside. Inside it's just you all alone with your damage. Outside, as people leer and whisper, does it somehow numb the pain? Numb you?

Does it harden you as you wrap yourself in scar tissue to protect yourself from all those curious eyes? All those wagging tongues?

Getting to my feet I push a hand through my hair and force the thought away.

Zoë was built small too. Like Blue. But she'd also stopped eating for the most part. She bore her scars on her own, on the inside. Well, she tried to tell me, but I neither heard nor saw. Not until it was too late.

My throat tightens, and I turn Blue's face away, so I don't have to see it. I tug the blanket over her. I can't feel sorry for her. She's blackmailing me. She has evidence that could be dangerous for me, if she's not lying, that is. If she truly has that duffel. But the fact that she knows about the bag at all is troubling. And then there's the hotel manager. I'll go over to see Jericho tonight, once I finish what I need to do here.

On the nightstand are the two things I brought over with me. A collar and a thin, but strong chain. I pick them up and sit on the bed again, taking hold of the collar around Blue's neck. It's part of the uniform at The Cat House. It's similar to the one the courtesans wear but this one is just for show, so I slip it off and replace it with the new one, a thin strip of leather, soft and malleable but strong. I lock it into place and through the D-ring between her collarbones, I slip the chain. I secure that to the bed with another lock and, after checking her new stitches, I set her hand on her stomach, palm up, and stand, smiling down at my handiwork.

A lesson in submission will go a long way. She needs to learn she is not in control. I am. She needs to understand that there are consequences to fucking with a man like me. And until I figure out exactly what she has on me, she will need to learn to heel.

Just one last thing I need to do before I leave my little convict to sleep. From my pocket, I retrieve her phone. I swipe to bring the screen to life then bend down to brush Blue's hair back before holding it up to her. Facial recognition. Much less secure than a pin code, actually. A moment later, I'm in. I smile as I add my own face to her phone, giving myself access to everything before removing her access altogether. I walk out of the bedroom switching out the light and closing the door behind me. I pocket her phone. I'll go through the little convict's life after.

A familiar, old gloom settles over me as I make my way through the dark corridor to the stairs and down and out the front door.

Because there's something I need to do.

Someone I need to visit now that I'm back.

8

EZEKIEL

The grounds are damp, although it's not raining anymore. My shoes will be ruined. It doesn't matter, though.

I walk guided by memory. The Bishop and St. James properties stand back-to-back. When Jericho took over the Bishop house after Carlton's death, he had the wall between the properties brought down, uniting the vast grounds. Matty will be the inheritor of the estate but that won't happen until he's eighteen and he's far from that. But the real reason he did it isn't for Matty, who's too young to know anything about the history between our families. He did it for his wife, Isabelle. She, too, is a Bishop. Ironic how life plays with us. He vowed to destroy the Bishop name, to wipe it from the face of the earth and here he is putting babies in her belly. Babies that will bear his name.

Love is a strange thing.

I stop.

Love.

I can't remember the last time I've used the word. Given it any thought at all.

With a shake of my head, I continue on, the bottoms of my pants sodden from the damp earth. At least Jericho is maintaining the gardens.

It takes a little bit but soon I see the lights of the St. James house. It was my home once. It doesn't belong to me anymore. I'm not sure it ever did. I was more of a caretaker until my brother returned. It was always going to be his. He's first-born. And I don't begrudge him that. That house holds far too many ugly memories for me, hanging my failures in front of me almost as if to remind me. As if I could forget.

From here, I see the curving path leading from the edge of the Bishop line to where the St. James property starts. I cross the now invisible barrier and push my hands into my pockets, the air damp and chilly. I make my way not to the house but take a turn toward the small graveyard on the property. It's just for the family.

The chapel's tabernacle lamp burns inside, it's red glow visible through the narrow slit of a window as I approach from the side. I'm glad to see the graves are maintained, the small fence that had been rotting has been replaced. I enter through the gate, which doesn't creak like it used to, and stop, taking in the fresh flowers that stand in two spots. I should have brought something, I think too late.

I walk to the first one. Kimberly's grave. The stone has recently been cleaned and the flowers are fresh. I crouch down to look at it, brushing off a little bit of dirt. Kimberly is Angelique's mother. She and Jericho were engaged when she was killed while pregnant with Angelique. Her death was the catalyst that changed his life in ways I don't think he ever knew it would.

But she's not who I'm here to see. She never belonged to me and truthfully, I never belonged to her, either. Kimberly was always Jericho's.

I straighten, wipe off my hands and turn to the Mausoleum wall. It takes me a moment, the guilt that had grown subtler in the last two years that I've been away taking on its old, familiar sensation, a twisting presence in my gut. A weight on my chest. I grit my teeth and force a smile as if she could see me. I approach the wall where the second small bouquet of wildflowers is. My throat tightens as I get closer, and I glimpse something different. Something new. There's a small photograph of her. Zoë. It wasn't here before.

Three years I've been away. Three years I haven't been to visit my sister. There's a hole where our father's bones had been resting too close to hers. It was wrong for him to be close to her in death when she did what she did to escape him in life.

Jericho did that when he learned the truth. I should have done it myself. I should never have allowed him to be interred near her, but I couldn't, not without telling the world what he'd done.

Too late I found out. Too late I saw. She was long gone by then.

He paid in the end. I collected on my sister's behalf. It wasn't nearly what he deserved.

I take in an audible breath of cold, damp air and tell myself to get it together. Zoë has been dead longer than she was alive. She was just sixteen when I found her. My sister. My twin. The person I was supposed to have an unbreakable bond with. A connection deeper than any other. But still, I didn't see it. Not when it was right in front of my eyes.

I touch the marker of her name then shift my gaze to the photograph. I wonder why he did it. It must have been Jericho. Or maybe it was our mother. But I find I'm glad it's here. Glad to see her like this. Like she'd been before. Young and happy. Although it's bittersweet.

"I'm sorry I've been away so long," I say.

There is no answering breeze. No chill to raise the hairs on the back of my neck. There was, once, but she's gone. I should take comfort in that, perhaps. Knowing that she's at peace. But I don't deserve comfort. Even after what I did, punishing the man who put her in her grave far too early, I don't deserve comfort. I need to remember her and along with her memory, my own failure.

"Thought you'd make your way out here."

I turn to find Jericho standing with an umbrella. I realize it's started to rain. He steps closer, shielding us both from the rain.

"I like the photograph," I say.

He looks at it, smiles. "That was mom. It's good to remember her that way." He turns his gaze to me, studies me. "You shouldn't have stayed away so long, Zeke."

"I'm not back, Jericho. Not to stay."

He looks like he's going to say something but, after a long moment, nods. "The girl?"

"Asleep."

"Come to the house. They all went to bed hours ago. No one will see you."

"I should get back. I have to prepare things."

"We need to talk. I'm a part of this too, remember."

That he is, especially considering what Blue told me about where she got her information. I nod and we walk to the house in silence. I'm not sure how I feel seeing it again. I lived here most of my life but it's not home. I don't have a home.

We walk in through the doors at the back and, as he said, the house is dark and quiet. I recognize the smell of the place and breathe it in. Every house has a smell that belongs to it. It's made up of lives being lived and memories of the past, good and bad.

He shakes out the umbrella and sets it aside. I follow him into the study. The desk lamp is on as is the one beside the couch. I take in the old, familiar space, noting he hasn't changed much.

"Whiskey?"

I nod, taking a seat on the couch. He brings over the bottle and two tumblers, pours, then sits on the leather armchair across from the sofa.

"You must be tired," he says.

"I am." I'm jet lagged but my plan wasn't to stay long enough to adjust to the time difference. I was going to handle Blue and get out of town before anyone found out I was even here. But things have changed. She isn't what I expected.

My phone buzzes in my pocket alerting me to a text. I take it out and read it. It's from Robbie.

Robbie: Check your email.

That's all. No odd remark, no jokes. Just a straightforward text.

"What is it?" Jericho asks.

"Robbie."

I set my drink down and click into my email. I open the first of several attachments. It's a photo of a woman about Blue's age but it's not her. Although if I look closely, there's some resemblance in the particular shade of blue of the eyes, in the slant of the nose. This woman, though, has blond hair and pale skin. Blue's natural hair color is dark, and her skin has an olive tint.

I peer closer. There's something strange in the woman's expression. Something absent.

Jericho comes to sit beside me and looks over my shoulder.

"Who is that?"

I scroll down and read her name. Wren Thorne. Age 21. Resident of Oakwood Care Facility, admitted half a year ago. Attached to it is a copy of a check written by B. Thorne.

Thorne.

Not Smith. Not that I believed it was.

"I think that's Blue's sister." I scroll back up to look at her photo again.

"Oakwood," Jericho says.

"Medical facility. Their patients are mostly children and adults who have sustained a brain injury."

Another email comes in just as my phone rings. I glance at the display and answer.

"I'm not waking you, am I?" Robbie asks, again no joking in his tone.

"Nope. What is this?"

"Figured it'd be easier to call and explain. That picture is of Wren Thorne. Or at least that's the name on the documents used to admit her to the Oakwood Care Facility as well as the facility she was at before that in sunny Orlando, Florida."

"She's Blue's sister," I say.

"Half right."

"What does that mean? Wait, I'm putting you on speaker. My brother's here. You remember Jericho?"

"Sure do. Hey Jericho, how are you doing?"

"All right. You?"

"Fine. Enjoying Amsterdam."

"Robbie," I say, getting him back on track.

He clears his throat. "The last name, though, it's not hers. The documents used to admit Wren were forged. Well, at least tampered with. I just sent you another email. I marked where the last name was doctored and honestly not very well."

"The checks, B. Thorne. Is that Bluebird Thorne?"

"No, the account belongs to a Bethany Thorne and the only transactions over the last two years are checks written to Oakwood where Wren is living now. Before that, they were written to the facility in Florida. Just sent those your way."

"Who's Bethany Thorne?"

"Bethany Thorne is Wren's mother. The address, Philadelphia address by the way in case I didn't mention it. Anyway, the address on the checks is where Wren and Bluebird a.k.a. Blue Masterson, lived. Thing is, Bethany Thorne disappeared four years ago. Whoever is using the account, and my guess is it's Blue, makes cash deposits in the same amount as the checks that are written monthly. Now on to you being half right about Wren being Blue's sister. Bethany Thorne was married three times, last time to a Thomas Thorne. Now he sounds like a real winner. According to Wren's birth certificate, though, he's not her father. Her father is James Johnson, Bethany's husband at the time of Wren's birth. They divorced shortly after, and Bethany married Thorne. She had his child, Bluebird, two years after Wren's birth. I attached her birth certificate."

"So they're half-sisters?"

"Yep. Thomas, or Lucky Tommy as he likes to be called these days, although Unlucky might be more apt, considering his current circumstances, is Blue's father but not Wren's. Bethany, however, was lucky. For a time. She's in the paper for having won three hundred thousand in the lottery a few years back."

"Well, good for her."

"And, surprise of surprises, that's when Tommy, who'd been gone for some time, moved back in. I guess the money made him realize how much he loved his wife and daughter."

"Sounds like it."

"A few months after that, Bethany disappeared. You catching on?"

"Yeah. Sounds like a gem. Where is Lucky Tommy now?"

"Prison."

I glance at Jericho, my eyebrows rising. "What put him there? Did they find Bethany?" Jericho asks.

"No, she's still a missing person. Someone called in a tip on an armed robbery and police picked him up at a strip club near their home. Timing is interesting. Wren's brain injury came a few years ago. Evidence turned up out of thin air a few days after her mental condition was diagnosed. Poor kid. She'd been accepted to medical school before things took a turn for her."

"Did she have an accident or something?"

"Or something. Blue took her to the hospital. There are photos of both girls. I'll send those your way as soon as I can. Police got involved but Blue swore they'd fallen down the stairs."

"Both of them?" Jericho asks.

"Mhm."

"And did a window break Blue's fall and give her that nasty cut across her face?"

He snorts.

My chest tightens, my hand clenches, unclenches.

"Anyway, Lucky Tommy was never arrested for it. Not even sure cops ever questioned him. At least, not for that. However, the night he was picked up for robbery, the girls disappeared. Took mom's car and got out of town. They've been MIA ever since. Until now, of course."

"How bad is Wren?"

"It doesn't look like she'll ever make a full recovery. I'll dig into more details on her if you like?"

"Yeah. Do," I say, not sure why. I ignore my brother's raised eyebrows.

"There's one more thing you need to know now, though."

"What's that?"

"Lucky will be up for parole soon."

"How? Doesn't armed robbery carry a longer sentence than three years?"

"Made a deal with prosecutors turning in an associate of his. Turns out Lucky wasn't holding the gun."

"But none of this answers the question of how this Blue Masterson or Thorne or whatever her name is got her hands on the information she's using to blackmail my brother," Jericho says.

"I'm still digging into that. I will tell you this. You're not her first mark. She's done this twice before and I am thinking it's how she was able to pay for her sister's medical care and house and feed herself at sixteen, seventeen, eighteen."

"And here I thought I was special. Keep digging and send me everything as you get it. Send whatever you have on Lucky too, will you?"

"Will do. You boys should get some sleep," he says more casually.

We say goodbye and disconnect the call. I pick up my whiskey and sip it.

"What did you find out from her?" Jericho asks.

"Well, she says she got her information from the hotel manager you spoke with over in Austria."

"What?"

"Turns out he held onto the duffel I'd thrown away."

"That piece of shit."

"Yeah, well, I'm not saying I believe her just yet so sit tight. No impromptu trips to Austria. But maybe let's track him down."

"That's a good idea. What's your plan?"

"I have her phone. I'll go through it in the morning and see what I find."

"And she's asleep now?" he asks, eyebrows raised. "Just decided to take a nap?"

"With a little help."

"Anyone going to miss her?"

"I don't think so. Apart from her sister, at least." I stand. "I'm tired."

He gets to his feet, too, and nods. "Let me know what I can do, okay?"

"I will. Goodnight, brother."

"Night."

9

BLUE

I wake up to pain. I groan, trying to force my eyes to open as consciousness slowly creeps in and I remember why my hand is throbbing, but not sure why my head is. I finally manage to peel my eyelids back and I find myself staring up at an unfamiliar ceiling, the weight of a warm, heavy duvet over me. I lift my arm which makes the pain worse and study the neat little row of stitches in my palm and the night comes back to me slowly, in reverse.

That bottle of whiskey on the table. My empty glass. My hand on his lap, his thigh warm and strong, his hands confident as he sewed me up.

Nausea roils my insides when I recall the image of the needle going through my skin. Second time in my life I've had to get stitches without any kind of numbing agent. Shouldn't there be some cap on that sort of thing? Or is karma just really out to get me?

I remember talking. A lot. What was I telling him? It had all grown strangely, and wrongly, comforting. How?

But then I recall what he'd said when I'd fallen over and he'd caught me. Not to drink something given to you by your enemy.

He drugged me. The fucking bastard drugged me.

I need to get up. Figure out where I am. I turn my head, hear an unfamiliar sound when I move as I take in the room. It's not the one he put me in when he brought me here. This one is opulently furnished, luxurious, the duvet heavy and warm, the pillow beneath my head soft. Did he tuck me in? I shake my head at the thought and take in the elegant neutral tones. I can imagine the money that's gone into this place.

The drapes on both windows stand open and bright sunlight pours in.

Startling realization dawns on me. Wren. What time is it? Did I sleep through the night? I never sent my sister the second part of the knock-knock joke. She'd have waited for it. It's not morning anymore. I can tell that from the bright light. I always call her in the morning.

I bolt upright. Except as soon as I'm about half-way up, something seizes my throat, and I realize what that sound of moments ago was.

I'm collared. I'm fucking collared and chained to the bed by my neck!

"What the fuck?"

The chain is short, forcing me to keep my head bent when I turn to look at where it's attached to a rung of the bed. The blanket falls away as I shift my position, and it's at that point I realize I'm completely naked, dried blood still smeared on my skin from my hand. At least, I think it's from my hand.

I peer down between my legs. No. No blood there. With an exhale, I take mental inventory, but nothing apart from my hand and head hurt. He didn't touch me, not like that. I don't think he would have. It's not him.

The thought of my mind deciding he's too good a human being to touch me while I'm out cold is unsettling to say the least. He only sewed me up so I wouldn't bleed out in his house because he needed me to answer his questions. He needs me right now. That's all. Once he has the information he needs, what will he do with me? Let me walk away? I doubt it. What will happen to Wren if something happens to me? They'll put her in some crappy under-funded state institution. There's no way I'll allow that.

I tug at the chain. It's thin but has no give. I can't break it. I slip my finger under the collar. I should be able to get it off. It just snaps into place usually. But then I notice the one thing of mine he left in the room. The collar that goes with my uniform. It's on the nightstand.

"Zeke!" I call out as loud as I can. I don't get a response, so I do it again. My head throbs but I push through the pain. I turn to face the headboard fully to give the chain some slack as I examine it. Patience has never been my forte and I grip it again, my one hand useless when it starts to bleed a little. I get up on my knees and grip the rung I'm bound to. I'm forced to lean forward because the chain is so damn short. I tug at the chain, then, when nothing happens, I shake the rung.

"Now that is a sight I can get used to," says a low, deep voice I'm starting to hate.

I look back over my shoulder to find Ezekiel St. James

standing in the doorway. He's leaning against the frame, casually sipping from a cup of coffee, and grinning that sly asshole grin of his. He's just watching me.

Watching my bare ass which is fully on display in my current position bent over as I try to break myself out.

"You asshole! You fucking drugged me!"

I drop to a seat, turn to face him while trying to gather up the blanket that has slid to the floor so I can at least cover myself.

"Is asshole really the only word you can come up with? It's getting boring, Bluebird."

It's startling to hear him call me by my full name. That name belongs to a different life. Then I remember giving it to him. What did I say my last name was? Smith?

"Untie me! Now!" I demand.

He chuckles, casually walks in. "You don't give the orders, sweetheart." He puts his coffee on the nightstand and digs two pills out of his pocket. "For the pain." He holds them out to me.

"No, thank you! I'm not going to willingly swallow your drugs!"

"Advil," he says. "Take them."

"No."

"Suit yourself." He sets them on the nightstand, and I'm tempted, because everything hurts, but I don't touch them.

He bends to pick up the heavy duvet which I only managed to get a corner of and sets it on my lap, then sits down beside me. He smells fresh and looks well-rested. His five-o'clock shadow is trimmed to perfection, his dark hair neatly combed back. He smells clean, of expensive soap and aftershave with hints of sandalwood and leather and why the fuck am I breathing him in?

"What are you going to do to me?"

His gaze skims over me. "Anything I want."

I try to keep my expression neutral as I swallow, my heart pounding so hard I'm sure he can hear it.

"You're mine now, Little Convict. You belong to me."

"You drugged me," I say after a beat, unable or unwilling to think about what that means. I take in his clothing, a pair of jeans and a button-down shirt of which he's left the top button undone and has the sleeves rolled up to his elbows. My gaze catches on the tattoos circling both forearms. Twin snakes?

"Occupational hazard? You've done this before, right?" he asks.

I jut my chin out in response. How does he know?

"Back to your ass. I have to say, as a connoisseur, you do have an exceptionally lovely backside."

I drag my gaze up to his. Fury roils inside me, boiling my blood at his casualness, his nonchalance. All I can do in the face of this is raise my arms, make a fist of my good hand, and attack.

He laughs, catches both wrists. "Settle down. Feisty little convict, aren't you?"

"This isn't a fucking joke! I'm not playing some stupid game—"

"Neither am I, sweetheart," he says, tone serious as he squeezes my wrists. "Calm the fuck down."

"My sister!" I remember suddenly. "That man. Dex? What did he do?" I tug to get free of him.

"Take it easy."

"I answered your questions. You said if I—"

"I said take it easy. She's fine. Wren's fine."

He knows her name. I didn't tell him her name. I know that. I wouldn't have.

"Dex did not even enter the facility," he continues casually, switching his grip to keep both of my wrists in one of his hands and reaching into his pocket to take out his phone.

No. Wait.

It's not his phone he's taking out. It's mine!

He whistles some tune and starts scrolling. I drag my gaze up to his. "How the hell did you get my password?"

"I guess you're not the only one who's learning how to hack into people's lives and getting your hands on things that don't belong to you," he says, no mocking laughter in his expression this time. I keep my mouth shut. "Face ID. You can add that to your repertoire, I suppose."

"Give me my phone."

"Say please."

"Please give me my fucking phone."

"For a pretty girl you have a very ugly mouth."

That makes me stop momentarily because if there's one thing I know, it's that I'm not pretty. Not with the slash across my face.

When he releases my hands, though, I come back to what's important. I flip him off after he tosses the phone onto my lap. I pick it up, keeping my arms pinned to my sides so the blanket doesn't slide off.

He takes my damaged hand, surprising me with his gentleness as he studies the stitches. "Take it easy with this hand," he says seriously, and, keeping hold of it, he takes out some of the things I saw in the suturing kit from his pocket. I watch, surprised yet again by this man's actions when he rips the packaging off an alcohol swab and pats the skin around the stitches, cleaning it. "I mean it," he says, letting me pull my hand away. "You need to let that heal. You don't want me to have to re-do those stitches."

I turn my attention to my phone and realize why he was so easy about handing it over. When I hold it up to my face, it doesn't recognize me. When I try to punch in my passcode, I understand exactly what he's done. He took over my phone. And he didn't simply add his credentials to it but he removed mine altogether so I can't access my own phone.

Stupid Face ID.

I drop the phone onto my lap and look up at him, tugging the blanket closer. His gaze is sharp, intent, and I remember how it felt to have my hand resting on his hard thigh. How he worked so deftly at stitching me up. How relaxed and confident he'd been. When I recall his fingers on other more intimate parts of my body, my face heats up. I clear my throat and glance away, reminding myself that I am his prisoner. That he is my enemy. Not to mention he is a man who can easily overpower me. Isn't the chain at my throat evidence of that? I should be using my energy to figure out how to extricate myself from this situation, not get all freaking swoony over my kidnapper's skillful suturing skills. Christ. What is wrong with me?

"I need to use the bathroom."

"And you need a shower." Before I can respond, he reaches down to unlock the chain from the bed.

I gather up the comforter which is too heavy to lug along and contemplate how I'm going to get up off the bed and make it to the bathroom while I keep myself covered. He smiles that arrogant smile which I guess is more like a smirk. I swear, his composure through all this is the most unsettling thing.

He lifts my chain *like I'm a dog.*

"Come, Blue," he says like a man would say *to his dog* as he readies to take it for a walk. To add insult to injury, he makes some sound like a *gitty up.*

"I'm not your pet."

"You should be so lucky. Up. Or down on all fours is fine too. It might be my preference, actually."

I get to my feet, tugging the duvet around myself. I take a step but stop because I'm caught. I glance down and I'm very sure the toe of his shoe didn't accidentally step on a corner of the blanket. I meet his eyes, give him a glare. He just smiles like he has no idea. I have no choice but to drop it. He shrugs a shoulder and begins to walk toward what I guess must be the bathroom and I stumble behind him, *my lead* too short.

When we get to the bathroom, he walks me inside, follows me and only then does he close the door. Only problem is he's on the wrong side of it.

He releases my chain, and it drops heavy and cool between my breasts. His gaze follows its movement as it sways then settles before his eyes return to mine.

"Go on," he says. "Use the bathroom."

I raise my eyebrows. "What? Are you going to watch?"

He grins.

"No. No way. Get out."

"I'm not going anywhere."

I grit my teeth. "Please get out."

"Aww. I think you may have a sweet side after all. But no."

I exhale, muster all my strength and stride toward him. He watches my approach, my leash, my fucking leash swinging like a pendulum between my breasts, the lock hanging off the end of it brushing my clit with each step. It's cold and I don't like the sensations it's sending through me as the weight of it swings back and forth.

A sound comes from inside his throat as he openly takes me in.

I take a long look at him. He's tall, well over six feet. He's broad shouldered and although not bulky, I see the definition of muscle in his shoulders and biceps through his shirt. I take in the twin tattoos, the scaly flesh of what might be snakes or dragons maybe circling his arms. I wonder where they meet.

But it's not that that has me grin as I lift my gaze to his and tilt my head. Because his eyes have gone dark, and a glance down reveals the outline of his erection.

I change tactic and give him a wide grin. "You like looking at me, Zeke?" I ask in my most seductive voice which honestly probably isn't very.

"It's Ezekiel. We're not friends."

"No, we're not." I get closer, close enough to slap my hand over his erection and squeeze. He's surprised, very clearly, and I relish the moment of victory even knowing he'll punish me for it. "But tell me, do you like looking at me, *Ezekiel*? I get the feeling you do," I say, squeezing, sliding my hand up and down.

He exhales with what I can only call a deep, almost animal rattle from inside his chest and brushes a knuckle over my cheek. When I jerk my head away, he chuckles and next thing I know, he hooks his finger through the ring at the center of my choker and hauls me up on my tiptoes by it. This close, I can see the interlocking rings of black and silver that circle his eyes and feel the heat coming off his skin. I inhale, taking in his aftershave, the leathery, clean scent of him. He draws me nearer, and I set my free hand on his shoulders for balance. I swallow then lick my lips. His eyes narrow when they settle on my mouth. He leans close enough that the stubble on his cheek tickles my face. I hear his soft intake of breath, as if he's inhaling my scent. And when he speaks, warm air brushes my ear making me shiver. Making the hairs on the back of my neck stand on end.

"I like looking at you very much, Bluebird Thorne," he says in that low, slow tone of his, the deep timbre of his voice a vibration that passes from his chest to mine. "But do you know what I like even better?"

I swallow again, my heart thudding against my ribcage.

"Your hand squeezing my cock." I gasp when he licks the shell of my ear before he drags his teeth over the lobe. Blood pulses through me, my nipples tightening to peaks and moth wings fluttering inside my stomach. "I think I'd like your pretty lips around it even more." As he says it, he draws back to look at me and holds my gaze as he begins to push me down to the floor by the collar. "Yes, I think I'd like to see you on your knees with my cock fucking that dirty little mouth of yours. What do you think, Little Convict?"

I shake my head, pull my hand from around his erection and grip his arm, digging my fingernails into it though his shirt.

"Never. Let me go," I tell him, recovering myself but just barely. I'm flushed red, I'm sure. I can feel the heat of my body's betrayal on my face, and I have no doubt he can see clearly how he's affecting me.

"Never say never. Don't you know that?" He jerks me upright and this time, he doesn't bring his mouth to my ear. This time, we're nose-to-nose and the darkness inside his wolf eyes sends alarm bells ringing.

There's a beast inside this man with his elegant, refined façade. And I've woken it.

"Let me go."

"If you don't want to suck my cock, then you shouldn't be wrapping your hands around it, should you?"

"Let me go."

"I asked you a question."

"Just let me fucking go."

"Answer my fucking question," he says through his teeth.

"No. No I guess I shouldn't. Maybe you should keep your eyes in your head then. Or better yet. Give me my clothes back!"

"Not a quick learner, are you?" he asks, releasing me abruptly so I stumble backward. "Piss, Blue."

"What?"

"You said you needed to, so do it. Then you can shower, and I can get on with my business."

I gesture to the door for him to go.

He cocks his head like he doesn't understand.

"You're not watching me."

"You lost all your rights to privacy when you decided to blackmail me." He checks his watch. "You have one minute. I'm a busy man."

"I'm fine. I don't need to go."

"Suit yourself. Get in the shower."

"I'm not showering while you watch either."

"You need to get the blood off you."

"I wouldn't be bleeding if it wasn't for you."

"You wouldn't be here at all if you hadn't decided to blackmail me. In. Now."

I think it may be stupid, but I dig my heels in and shake my head.

"No? Okay, how about this." He takes a step toward me. "Let's learn lesson number one." He takes another step and I have to take one back. "We'll change roles, shall we?"

"What does that mean?"

"I'll be the blackmailer and you be the blackmailee. Is that a word?"

"What are you talking about?"

"Your sister left you a voice message. She sounds sweet."

"What?"

"A knock-knock joke she's waiting on?"

I feel my face pale.

He raises his eyebrows. "You should really text Wren back. And honestly, I'm curious myself. I mean, who doesn't love a good knock-knock joke?"

"Give me my phone."

"Step into the shower."

"Give me my phone." I wipe away a stupid traitor tear.

"Into the shower. You'll piss. Then you'll wash yourself and when I'm satisfied, you may tell Wren the rest of that joke. You left her hanging on a cliff, Blue. That's not very nice, considering her mental state—"

"Go to hell!" I scream and fling myself at him.

He catches me easily, gripping my arms and backing me into the glass wall of the shower. The tips of his shoes brush my bare toes.

"No, sweetheart, you go to hell. What's happening here and now? That's all your own doing. Tell me something. How does it feel, Little Convict? Being blackmailed? Having someone else take control of your life?"

"This is different. Wren's... sick."

"So, do as you're told, and you can message her."

He's determined. He's teaching me a lesson. And he's not going to let me off the hook. So, I do as he says and step into the shower.

"Happy?" I ask.

"Not yet."

I look at him over my shoulder.

"Face me."

"Why?"

"You know what you have to do."

"Zeke, I—"

"Ezekiel. We're not friends, remember. Face me."

I do.

"You wanted to use the bathroom. So, squat and do it. While I watch."

I swallow. He's going to make me do this. In front of him. He's going to humiliate me like this.

"Squat, Blue, and piss. Then you can text your sister."

I stare up at him, my heart racing. "You're sick," I say through gritted teeth even as my eyes fill with hot tears. I can't back down, though. I can't cower. It's what he wants.

She shrugs a shoulder.

"Will it get you off?" I ask and it's a mistake, I know the instant the words leave my mouth because he's on me before I can blink, before I can get away. He grabs a fistful of my hair and tugs my head backward, his predator's eyes searching my face, settling too long on my mouth.

"I'm a little more complicated than that." He tightens his fist in my hair forcing tears to burn the corners of my eyes. "Squat and piss," he says, forcing me down. Once I'm squatting, he steps away, his gaze locked on mine.

And I do it. I look up at him, having to force myself to hold his gaze, to not look away even as my face burns and I do it, feeling the warm liquid against my thighs and Ezekiel St. James watching me, degrading me with his cool expression even as a tear slides down my cheek.

Only when I'm finished do I look away because I can't hold his gaze anymore.

"Good girl. That wasn't so bad, was it?" I don't answer. "Stand up." He takes my phone out of his pocket and unlocks it. I stand, wipe my tears, closing my eyes when I hear Wren's voice playing her part, asking 'who's there?' in three repeated, increasingly anxious voice texts.

"Who's there, Blue?" Ezekiel asks and I wipe my nose with the back of my hand and reach for the phone. He hands it over and it takes me a minute to get myself under control. I do it for her. I have to do it for her. If I'd been there, if I hadn't dragged my feet because I didn't want to be home, maybe I would have made it back in time. The difference was minutes. Minutes and she'd be the big sister I remember. But she's not. And she never will be again.

"Blue," he says.

I swallow over the lump in my throat and try to block out the ringing in my ears. I hit the record button. "Beets," I say, hoping she won't hear the trembling of my voice. I hit send and watch the second arrow show up, telling me it's been delivered. I see the time. It's almost four in the afternoon. She'll be at her physical therapy session. She'll get it soon though.

I turn to find Ezekiel watching me and the look in his eyes is not what I expect. Not at all. I hold the phone out. "She'll text me back. And then I can give her the answer."

He nods once, pockets the phone and it's like all that aggression, all that hate, has gone out of him and we're both just standing there, two hollowed-out husks that maybe were once human beings.

"I'll keep an eye on it," he says, then pauses and for a minute, I think he's going to say something more and I'm not sure what I want but then he changes his mind and turns and leaves.

I exhale and suck in a ragged breath. I switch on the shower and stand under the flow, and I sob.

That did not go as planned.

The lock on the bathroom door clicks behind me. I would expect no less. I hear the shower switch on as I walk out of the bedroom, one of the spare rooms in Carlton Bishop's massive house, and lock the door behind me. She doesn't run after me calling out or banging on the door, demanding release, but I don't expect that. Not after that exchange. She's in there licking her wounds. It's what I wanted. To make her heel. And I achieved my goal. I need to keep her under control. What I didn't expect was to lose control. Which I did.

I stop in the hallway and force a deep breath in.

She was right. I do like looking at her. I can't quite put my finger on why. She's attractive, yes, but so are many other women. Women I have easy access to. Women I can do what I please with and walk away from. The Cat House alone is full of them. So, what the fuck is my problem? Why did I let her get to me?

I need to keep my head on straight. Blue has evidence

that can destroy me and my brother in the process. What just happened needed to happen. She needs to understand that she cannot cross a man like me. I'm doing the only thing I can do.

Guilt gnaws at me as I force myself to continue down the hall. Her sister is mentally damaged. I don't like the idea of using her. It doesn't feel right.

When I get downstairs, Dex walks in the front door carrying a suitcase.

"Ezekiel," he says in greeting. "Morning."

"Morning," I say. It's not that I dislike Dex. I don't feel either way about him. He is my brother's trusted right-hand man. If I'm honest, I may be a little jealous of that as idiotic as it sounds.

"All good here?" he asks, handing me the keys to the Range Rover. It's my car and I've kept it at the house while I've been in Amsterdam.

"All good." I hand him the key to Blue's bedroom. "That's from Isabelle?" I gesture to the suitcase.

He nods. "Everything you asked for." I asked Jericho to send some of Isabelle's clothes for Blue. They're about the same size.

"And then some," I say, having expected a few things. "Put them in her room, will you? She's having a shower."

Dex nods. "Jericho's sending Cynthia over too." Cynthia worked as part of the household staff while Jericho was away. "She'll be here soon."

"Good." I walk into the kitchen where I find Blue's purse on the counter. I'd already emptied out its contents but found nothing interesting. I pick up the ring of keys.

"Thanks. I'm heading to the apartment. I'll be back in

a couple hours." I walk out the door and into the SUV. I've missed it. I've missed a lot of things these last few years.

Once Jericho and Isabelle's relationship shifted and the Bishop threat was removed, it was time for me to leave the St. James house, my childhood home, that I'd been living in all those years Jericho was hiding Angelique. Strangely, although leaving numbed some of the pain of the past, being away also has forced me to focus on it from a different angle.

The thing with Zoë, what happened with her, to her, what she did when she could no longer cope, all that pain is still there, has been all along. Somehow, I was able to mask it throughout those years. Maybe it was my mother's illness, maybe it was my brother and his secrecy around his daughter's existence. Maybe it was keeping up appearances, who the fuck knows? There was enough to occupy my mind that I could bury my own shit.

That all changed when Isabelle moved into the house and maybe it had to do with my brother finding happiness. Maybe it was that that pushed me out because all of a sudden, all those things I'd buried deep were right there, confronting me at every fucking turn of every fucking corner. Zoë's face. Memories of her the last years of her life. Not during the happy times, though. I seem to only remember the bad. The sad. Guilt, maybe, remembering her wasting away before my eyes and me just fucking missing it.

And there are the memories of our father, of course. The things he did to us. Mostly to her, I know now.

My mind shifts to what I learned from Robbie about

Blue's father. The damage he did to her and her sister. What is it with fathers? Aren't they supposed to protect their daughters? There are enough monsters in the world without having to be attacked in your own home by a man who should protect you, aren't there?

That sensation of my throat closing up, all that old emotion, the damage I'd been able to keep buried for so many years, it's back. Like it was toward the end of my time there. I close my eyes, force in a deep breath, tell myself to focus.

Amsterdam has helped, at least a little. I don't see Zoë's face at every turn. She was never there. My failure to protect my twin sister doesn't fucking stare me in the face every fucking minute of the day there. But it's not like I lived a life there either. I exist. What right do I have to live a life? How selfish for me to even consider it when she doesn't get to be alive at all?

My cell phone rings as I drive off the property. I push a button to answer, and Jericho's voice fills the car.

"Where are you?"

"I'm heading to Blue's apartment to see what I can find. Thanks for the clothes, by the way."

"I'll pass that on to Isabelle."

"You told her?"

"What was I going to do, go into her closet and take her clothes and hope she wouldn't notice? Speaking of, you left things here too. Guessing you'll need them. I'll bring them by later. Since you'll be spending more time here than you expected why don't you come over? See the kids. You're still Angelique's favorite uncle."

I chuckle. "Easy when you're the only uncle. What

was the manager's name at Hotel Petterhof by the way?" I ask, changing the subject.

"Spencer. Mitch Spencer. He's no longer employed at the property, but I've got someone looking into his whereabouts."

"Keep me posted."

"Pick me up. I'll go with you."

"No."

"I want to help, Zeke."

"No. You're not part of this. I'm not getting you involved any more than you already are. You work on finding Spencer. I'll call you once I leave the apartment."

"I don't like this."

"Join the club. I gotta go."

"All right, brother," Jericho says after a long silence. "I'm here for you whatever you need."

I nod, knowing he can't see me, and disconnect the call. I head toward Blue's apartment. I spent a few hours looking through her phone last night but didn't find much. She has no contacts apart from her sister and a contact marked Rudy Nurse who apparently works at the facility. No socials, as I already knew. Her web searches and history were meticulously cleared. And the only email in her inbox was the one notifying her of my one-dollar deposit into her account.

Her texts with her sister changed abruptly about two years ago. She only sends her knock-knock jokes. There are messages from Rudy, too, who gives her updates on how Wren is doing. How must it feel to not know your sister anymore even though she's right there? Is it a similar loss as death? In a way, it must be.

But I can't care about that. I need to focus on the task at hand. Like I told Blue, she's here because she fucked up. She has only herself to blame and I can't care about the motivator behind her attempt to blackmail me.

The apartment building is about forty-five minutes away in a pretty shitty neighborhood. When I arrive, I park my SUV in the lot and look around. It probably costs more than all the cars parked here combined. I climb out, lock it, and look up at the five-story building that looks like it hasn't had any work done to it in a decade at least.

In the corner of the lot, I see a worn-out Honda Passat, its black paint peeling, one of the tires looking like it needs air. The car stands out because it's the only one with Pennsylvania plates. I cross the lot to take a closer look, peering into the window when I find the doors locked. I'm pretty sure it's hers. I snap a photo of the license plate and send it to Robbie asking him to find out who it's registered to.

I head toward the stairs that will lead inside. One of the two glass doors at the entrance has a crack in it that's been taped up and the lock is broken. I push the door open and enter. The vestibule is messy with two broken umbrellas just lying on the floor and a bag of trash someone couldn't be bothered to take to the dumpster I saw in the corner of the lot. It stinks.

Breathing through my mouth, first thing I do is find Blue's mailbox. Using her key, I unlock it and take out the stash of mail, mostly circulars, a blank postcard of what looks to be a children's book titled Run Rabbit Run, and an electricity bill. Taking those, I head up to her apartment hearing televisions, a baby, a man and woman fighting along the way. The air in the hallways is stale, old food and B.O. Blue's apartment has a worn-out welcome mat at the door. I wonder if it's hers or if it was left here by the previous tenant. I unlock three locks and enter. Once inside, I close the door behind me and flip the light switch because even though it's daytime, all the blinds are down, and the apartment is dark. I take in the room.

First thing I notice is how neat everything is. The carpet is worn ragged, the furniture which consists of a sofa, a dining table with two chairs is mismatched and the TV is an ancient box. I wonder if it works. But contrary to the smells and look of the apartment building itself, this one smells of cleaning supplies.

Someone must use the sofa as a bed because a pillow and a folded blanket rest on one corner.

On the dining table is a notebook and a closed laptop. It's an old Apple. I open it and it comes to life, the cursor blinking in the space to enter a passcode. Above the empty space is the word Lucky. There's a picture of a young girl holding a kitten, trying to give it a lick of her ice pop. I peer close and I think it's Blue.

I won't bother trying various passwords and plan on taking it back with me.

The kitchen is tiny. It's meticulous apart from the pot in the sink with the single fork inside it. There's a box of cereal on the counter and a cereal bowl and spoon are in the drying rack.

I open the fridge and find it contains a container of milk and little packets of ketchup and mayonnaise. In the drawer are several apples.

From the kitchen I walk into the one bedroom. Inside is a neatly made twin bed and beside it the nightstand with a lamp on top. Nothing matches and it all looks old. In the closet, clothes hang neatly. I look through them, see the different sizes and style. Are some of these Wren's clothes? Has Blue kept them here?

On the nightstand is a framed photo. I pick it up, look at it. It's two girls and I recognize Blue, but she's got to be ten in here. The older girl must be Wren. They're standing on either side of a woman Blue resembles. Apart from the clothes, it's the only thing in the place that's personal. I get the feeling this is the one thing Blue would care about.

The bathroom is neat, with a small shoebox of makeup on a rack. Foundations and concealers as well as mascara and eyeliner.

There's a closet in the living room and I check in there, too, but only find a denim jacket on a hanger and a vacuum cleaner, a folded blanket on a high shelf, so I go back into the bedroom to look under the bed. There, shoved to the very back, is a backpack. Finally, something. I reach to drag it out and set it on the bed. I unzip it and inside, I find some clothes neatly folded, two baseball caps, a box of hair dye, blue. Surprise. At the bottom of the bag is a large envelope. I take it out, and inside find a wad of money.

All right. Now we're getting somewhere.

I count it. There is two-thousand dollars in cash here. I put it back and take out the smaller envelope. Inside that, I find a school ID. Wren Johnson. She must be sixteen or seventeen here. Used to go to Upper Darby

Senior High just outside of Philadelphia. Blue's is there too. She's a freshman so I guess about fifteen in the photo. I put both into the envelope and feel the bottom of the bag to see if I missed anything but find nothing.

Carrying the backpack, I walk back out into the living room and set it on the couch. I return to the kitchen to look through the cabinets for more, for something personal about Blue. Something regarding the evidence she has supposedly bought about me. Anything. The cabinets don't contain much apart from cleaning supplies under the sink, pasta and canned soup, salt and pepper are the extent of the spices. There's a bottle of olive oil. Several mismatched mugs, glasses and dishes fill up one cabinet. It's all kind of sad honestly.

This can't be it.

My phone buzzes alerting me to a message. I dig it out of my pocket and see it's a text from Robbie.

Robbie: Photos from the hospital.

I click to download the first. It's Wren, I think. Her face is badly bruised, her eyes black, one swollen shut, her hair, which is light blond, is darker here. Dried blood. She looks bad. Really bad.

I click into the next one. This one's Blue. She'd have been sixteen. Zoë's age. Her hair is long and dark, not yet blue, and she's wearing it loose. On her face is a bandage and it's bloody. There's a second photo of her and this one is without that bandage.

"Christ."

I see the stitches. They look as though they were done with a very shaky hand. Her own. I get it.

There are a few more photos and after glancing at

them, I put the phone back into my pocket. I want to know what happened. Why did Tommy beat them up so badly? Is this why they ran?

First, I need to wrap up here.

I go back to the living room and lift the folded blanket and pillow, check under the cushions of the couch. I don't even find a nickel or a crumb of food. The hall closet door is still ajar, and I return to it, lift the blanket off the top shelf and shake it out. I feel up on the shelf which is high for me so it would be too high for Blue to reach. I'm about to close the door when I look at the vacuum cleaner again, at the bag hanging from the back. It's an old upright and there's something heavy and awkwardly shaped in the bag. That or it's so old it's just lost its shape altogether. I pull it out of the closet and crouch down feel the bag with both hands and have a suspicion what it is that's got the bag looking so misshapen. I unzip the bag, turning my face from the dust to reach inside. My fingers close over a Ziploc bag. I pull it out, sneezing when dust gets in my nostrils. I look at what I've uncovered.

There, sealed in the Ziploc, is a revolver.

11

BLUE

When I come out of the bathroom, I find waiting for me a glass of orange juice and a suitcase. My stomach growls but first thing I do is check the door, which is still locked. I'm relieved. After what happened earlier, I'm not in a hurry to engage with Zeke.

I walk over to the nightstand and pick up the juice. It's freshly squeezed, and I drink it down, too thirsty not to. It won't be drugged. He has no reason to drug me now. My stomach growls, expecting food, but the juice will have to do. I go to the suitcase which sits open on a rack beside the closet and is full of women's clothes. They smell like they've just come from the laundry and a quick glimpse at a few labels tells me they're about my size.

I do wonder at the amount of clothes. Where did he get them? Are they trophies? Exactly how long is he planning on keeping me? I put the thoughts out of my mind as soon as they come and get to work. I'm still here. Still alive. And the way he was after what happened in the bathroom, when it came to my message to Wren, it gives me some hope. Maybe that's stupid but it's all I have.

I rummage through looking for underthings, tearing the suitcase apart, but come up empty. No panties and no bras. Is that by design? I also realize everything in here is either a dress or a skirt with a top. Not a single pair of jeans or pants at all. I'm suspicious as I choose an A-line skirt and a light top in pretty lilac, again, nicer than anything I own or have ever owned, and slip those on. It all fits like it was made for me. I tuck my leash underneath the top but am very aware of it rubbing up against my bare clit beneath the skirt, so I tug it back out and slip it into the pocket of the skirt. No one will see me in here anyway.

The ballet slippers are comfortable although they're half a size too big, but they'll work. Once I'm dressed, I look through the suitcase to see if there's a brush or makeup. I'm very aware of the scar on my face. It's not for the sake of vanity and it's not that I care how I look to Zeke, I just hate the scar and usually hide it beneath layers of foundation. But there's nothing like that in the bag and so I go into the bathroom to finger comb my hair. When I hear the key turn in the bedroom door, my heartbeat picks up and I grip the counter, looking straight ahead at my reflection. I take a deep breath in.

I can do this. I need to do this. I need to get through this so I can get to Wren.

Feeling a chill, I rub my arms before walking out of the bathroom and into the bedroom where I find Zeke holding a backpack.

I stare at that bag. And I want to cry.

Because him having it, it just takes one more option away from Wren and me.

He closes the door behind him.

I step fully into the bedroom.

He looks me over and I find myself tugging my hair down on the left side of my face. Habit. It takes me a minute to meet his eyes and instantly I feel a flush of heat at the memory of what happened earlier today. What he made me do.

But that's good for me. It forces me to muster my strength, to get it together, because I can't be embarrassed. I can't care. He's the one who should be embarrassed at how he treated me. What he made me do.

"Clothes fit?"

"There's no underwear."

"No?" he asks, very clearly not concerned.

Fine. "It's a lot of clothes. I don't plan on being here that long."

He makes some noncommittal sound.

"Where did you get them all anyway? Are they trophies or something?" I ask, trying for casual but failing.

"My brother's wife's clothes."

"She knows I'm here? That you're keeping me prisoner?"

He sets the backpack on the bed and unzips it. "Is this your go bag?" he asks, ignoring my question.

He begins to unpack it, taking out my laptop. Well, not actually mine but possession is 9/10ths of the law, right? I fold my arms and watch from my place, trying to keep my expression neutral as he empties out the contents, some clothes, shoes, jackets, baseball caps for Wren and me, the envelope of money and our old IDs.

"You got your electric bill," he says, laying what looks to be my mail on the bed as well. "And... Saved the best for last." He reaches into the bag again and draws out the Ziploc with the pistol in it.

The backpack was one thing but this? How did he find it? I feel the blood drain from my face at the sight and when the ringing between my ears starts, I reach for the edge of the nearest piece of furniture to stay upright but I find only air.

I stumble, but strong hands close over my arms to steady me.

"Easy, Blue."

I feel his warmth, the heat of his body. I set my hands on his chest, concentrating on breathing, and try to keep him at arm's length.

"I'm fine."

"You're not fine."

He's right, I'm not fine. I shake my head. I just need a minute. I let my fingers rest against his chest, feel the beating of his heart beneath the wall of muscle.

"Look at me."

"I'm fine." I feel queasy and if I had anything in my stomach, I'd probably have thrown it up.

"Blue?"

I force myself to open my eyes and it takes a moment for my pupils to focus, to see him clearly. He's so close. Why is he so close? Why is he looking at me like he is?

But then his eyes flit to the scar and I turn my face to hide it from him.

"What just happened? It's the second time I've seen you like that."

I give a shake of my head, extricate myself and put some space between us. "Nothing," I say, folding my arms across my chest.

"You stumbled. If I didn't catch you, you would have fallen."

"Well, aren't you the gentleman? Oh wait, you're not. Let me go. I'm fine."

He raises his eyebrows and I know he won't release me until I tell him.

"It's nothing. I just get a little dizzy now and then. It takes a minute, and it passes."

"What happens when you're driving, and it happens? Or you're at the top of the stairs?"

I give him a firmer shove. "I'm just hungry," I lie. "Low blood sugar." I pull free and take several steps away. "But it's touching that you care." I walk closer to the bed, eyeing the contents.

"Cynthia is preparing some food. We'll eat soon."

"Who's Cynthia?"

"Cook."

"She knows I'm here?"

He smiles. "She won't help you. No one will."

I study him. I know he's right. "Did Wren text back?"

"Not yet." He points to the bed. "Sit."

"Tomorrow's Sunday and it's her birthday."

"Is it?"

"I need to visit her."

"Do you?"

"She has a routine. She relies on it."

"I'm sure she does."

"How long are you going to keep me here?"

He smiles, cocks his head, and folds his arms across his chest. "You're blackmailing me. What do you think? I'm just going to let you walk away?"

I shiver with a sudden chill and rub my arms. No, he's not. He's not going to just let me walk away. Not when I can damage him.

"Let's focus, Blue. I need you to fill in some blanks for me." He steps closer, holds his phone out for me and when I look at it, I gasp with surprise. It's a photo of me. My face. It's from the night I took Wren to the hospital.

"Where did you get that?"

He scrolls through another of me then one of Wren.

When I see my sister, I look away.

"You took your sister to the hospital. You told them you fell down the stairs. Both of you. Police were called but you managed to convince them it was an accident, which is shocking, actually."

I keep my gaze averted. How does he know all this? Why does he know it?

"Is your father the staircase you both fell down?"

My gaze shoots up to his. How did he find out?

"Where did you get the two grand cash?"

I keep my mouth shut.

"Oh yeah, two other men you were extorting money from. That's right. Quite the leap to jump to 100K from me, isn't it?" He waits a beat and when I don't answer him, he continues. "No comment? Okay. Let's see how you do with the next one. Where is your mother, Blue?"

I blink away, pick the baseball cap that I bought for

Wren. She used to love baseball. She'd watch all the time. I never got it. This cap is her favorite team's. Although she doesn't remember that anymore.

"She got married a bunch of times, didn't she?" he prods.

I don't respond.

"Get around a lot, did she?"

At that, I leap up from my seat and slap my hands against his chest to shove him. "You don't get to say that! You don't get to say anything about her!"

He catches me easily, gripping my wrists and not letting go.

"I get to say anything I want." I try to tug free, but he holds tight, looks down at my injured hand. "I told you to take it easy with this." He walks me backward. "Now sit back down," he commands and deposits me on the edge of the bed.

"What do you want from me?"

"Truth. Your past. Your present. All of it. I want all of it."

"Why?" I'm confused, I don't understand why he cares to know so much. Something slips off the bed and my gaze automatically turns to it. It's the electric bill. Followed by something else.

A postcard.

My heart drops to my stomach as it floats down, landing face-up. I stare at it. Run Rabbit Run. The word *Blue* scrawled in barely visible tiny letters between the first Run and Rabbit.

"Are you listening to me?"

I blink, shift my gaze up to Zeke's. I guess he was talking. Probably still insulting my mother. I'm glad I didn't hear him.

"Where was this?" I ask, bending to pick it up. I turn it over and the words on the back make my blood run cold. "Happy Birthday, Wren. See you soon."

He found us.

Shit.

He found us.

No. I stop myself. He hasn't found her. Just me. He doesn't know where Wren is. He can't.

I turn it back over, see how the ink is smudged. I can almost make out the print from the pad of his hand. Where did he get the postcard? How does he get his hands on them? They don't sell those at the prison commissary, surely. My head spins. Did someone send it to him? He has contacts outside of prison. He always warned me about them.

"The gun. The serial number is filed off. Doesn't usually mean anything good," Zeke says.

I glance at it in its Ziploc, then at the postcard again. The little rabbit hopping. All the happy colors.

Zeke pulls the chair up to sit in front of me, close enough our knees are almost touching. My phone alerts me to a message. Well, the sound comes from his pocket, but I recognize the tone. It's Wren's.

He stops, takes it out of his pocket. Hits the button to play the audio.

Beet who? Wren asks and I can hear how she is enjoying the joke. My once brilliant sister who was going to be a doctor, a pediatrician because she loved kids. Backup plan was veterinarian because she also loved animals. She now finds entertainment in knock-knock jokes.

I want to cry.

"I hear she was accepted to medical school," he says, and I drag my gaze to his.

"How do you know all this?"

"I'm not like those other two you blackmailed. But I guess you've figured that out."

"Let me answer her." I hold out my hand.

"Answer me first. Is that gun yours?"

I shake my head.

"Who does it belong to?"

I look at his hand resting on his lap, study the colorful scales of the tattoo on one arm. "What is it?" I ask, not entirely sure why.

"What is what?"

I gesture to the tattoo.

He looks at it, like he forgot it was there. "Dragons."

"I thought they were snakes."

"The gun. Who does it belong to?"

I bite my lip, stare at the pistol, a 10mm with two cartridges containing fifteen rounds each.

"Is it your father's?"

I nod, although it's not true. I don't actually know the name of the man it belongs to and nodding is just easier.

"What happened to Wren? To your face?"

My hand instinctively moves to cover my scar. I take a deep breath, trying to keep it together.

"Tell me about that and you can text your sister."

It doesn't matter if he knows, does it? It just really

doesn't matter, and I don't have the energy to fight him, not on this.

"I came home late after school one day. Found Wren unconscious. He was holding her head underwater in the tub. I tried to get him off her and he hit me so hard I smashed the mirror over the sink with my face." I point to the scar. "He hit me again and I passed out. When I woke up, Wren was still in the tub, still unconscious. The water was freezing cold but at least she was breathing. He hadn't killed her."

"Your father?"

I nod. "He was angry about something. Scared maybe. I'd never seen him like that."

"Where was he when you woke up?"

"Don't know. Probably at the bar."

"You took her to the hospital?"

"Not then. I didn't realize what had happened to her. Two days later I took her. When she wasn't the same and I couldn't figure out what was wrong. And then, when I did, I got us out of there."

I'd been goofing off. I didn't want to go home, that's why I was late. I don't say that part out loud. My part in what happened to my beautiful, smart sister. My mistake that cost her so much.

He holds out the phone.

I take it, play my sister's message again. She sounds so young. I tell her the last of the joke. "Beets me," I say and hit send, then hand the phone back to him because the fight has gone out of me.

He takes it, tucks it into his pocket and stands. He

grabs the laptop, and the Ziploc then opens the bedroom door. "Come, Blue."

"Where?"

"Downstairs. You need to eat."

"Why?"

"So you don't have one of your dizzy spells at the top of the stairs."

"Don't want to clean up a mess?" I ask half-heartedly.

He gives me a weary smile.

"What happens after?"

He raises his eyebrows.

"What are you going to do to me?" I ask bluntly.

"You and I are going to come to an arrangement. For now. Up. You need to eat."

"What arrangement?"

"You have information that could hurt me, hurt those I care about. And I have something you need."

"What's that?"

"Protection." He must see my confusion. "From your father."

I blink, not quite understanding. "I need protection from you if anyone."

He smiles. "Isn't your father up for parole soon?"

My throat goes dry, and I clutch my stomach. "They won't let him out."

"How can you be sure?"

I shake my head. I can't be sure, but I have a plan if that happens. "Why would you want to help me?"

He shrugs a shoulder. "I guess I have a damsel in distress complex."

"I don't need some knight in shining armor to save me. I can save myself."

"Well, that's questionable. And the only knight I am is dark."

"Again, why would you help me?"

He shrugs his shoulder again. "I have selfish motives. You coming? You can stay here and starve, of course. Your choice."

I weigh my options. It's a quick decision because I have no options really. If I don't hear him out, I get locked back in and what? Nothing. Or I go with him, maybe make some deal. Some arrangement. He hasn't hurt me yet, not really. And if my father manages to get paroled, and he knows where I live, I'm going to need Zeke's protection. He just doesn't really know exactly what he'll be up against.

12

EZEKIEL

I lead the way downstairs, stopping in the study to drop off the laptop and the gun before heading into the kitchen. Cynthia is taking a casserole out of the oven as we enter the kitchen. When I smell the gnocchi in her signature sauce, my stomach growls.

"Cynthia, you remembered," I say, and she smiles. It's one of my favorite dishes.

"Of course I did. It's good to see you back, Mr. St. James."

She glances at Blue, giving her a polite smile before setting the casserole down on the counter.

"Would you like me to set a table?" she asks.

"No, that's all right. I'm sure my brother is anxious to have you back."

"I'll come in the morning then. Salad is in the refrigerator and don't worry about the dishes. I'll take care of it all tomorrow."

"Thank you, Cynthia."

"Goodnight."

"Am I invisible?" Blue asks once she's gone.

I gesture for her to take a seat at the counter where two plates are stacked.

"Cynthia understands the need for discretion." I find a serving spoon and heap some of the gnocchi onto one of the plates and Blue's stomach growls when I set it in front of her. "When was the last time you ate?" I ask as she digs in.

"Careful. I might think you care," she says, shoveling food into her mouth.

I grab the salad out of the refrigerator and carry over a bottle of wine Cynthia must have brought from the main house. I open it, pour two glasses. I set one in front of Blue and serve myself some of the gnocchi.

"No thank you," Blue says, pushing it away. "I learned my lesson."

"You saw me open it. It's not drugged."

"Nope."

I take her glass, sip from it and raise my eyebrows.

"I'm fine."

"Suit yourself. When was the last time you ate?"

"Before my shift at The Cat House."

"How did you know about The Cat House anyway?"

"Same way I knew about you."

"The Austrian guy?"

She nods, scratches her nose.

I smile, knowing this is her tell. She scratches the tip of her nose when she lies. She's completely unaware that she does it. "I doubt that. Was your father always abusive?"

Her fork stops half-way to her mouth, and she turns to me. "Why do you want to know?"

"I told you I want to know your past as well as your present. It's how I'll decide your future."

"I don't see why it matters but not to me, until that last night. He never hurt me before that. He mostly hurt Wren and mom. What arrangement do you want in exchange for protection?"

"Where is your mother?" I ask, ignoring her question.

She shrugs a shoulder and keeps her eyes focused on her plate.

"What caused your father to hurt you if he hadn't until then?"

"You'd have to ask him. All I know is not all fathers protect their daughters."

"I know that."

She looks up at me, studying me for a long moment. She sets her knife and fork down.

"Finished?" She nods and I get up. "Follow me." I lead the way to what must have been Carlton Bishop's study once. The fire is lit in the grate. It's a comfortable space with a desk against one wall and a sitting area that contains a sofa and well-worn leather chairs. I've placed a small, three-legged wooden stool that looks about a hundred years old in front of the fire.

"Is anyone else here?" she asks.

"Would it make you feel safer if there were?"

"Not really, no."

"No, it's just you and me."

"Is this your house?"

"No." She looks confused but I'm not here to answer her questions. "Sit." I point to the stool.

She looks at it, then at me, and rubs her arms like she's cold. "I'm fine."

"Sit anyway."

"Look, just tell me what you want from me, what arrangement. I'll do what you want and then I'll go. I'll get out of your life forever."

"That's not how blackmail works, sweetheart. Sit."

"I'll get rid of everything I have on you while you watch. Erase all the files—"

"Ah, but someone told me recently that not all things that get erased stay erased so that's not going to work for me." She opens her mouth maybe to protest, maybe to make some other promise, but I stop her. "I won't ask again, Blue."

She takes a deep breath in, exhales, then sits.

I pour myself a whiskey and take the seat on the armchair. I sip. "I assume you'll pass on the whiskey?"

She nods.

I set my drink down, pick up the laptop and turn it on. "Password?"

"FuckthePatriarchy. All one word. Capital F, capital P."

I glance at her and snort, then type it in and voila. I'm in. I don't even have to search to find a folder titled Z on the desktop. I glance at her, open it, and inside I see several photos and video files of myself at the hotel in Austria. The copies of the newspaper articles. I watch a video of my brother having a conversation with that asshole Mitch Spencer and after my brother leaves, I watch Spencer glance up at the camera as he takes a remote out of his desk, points it at the camera and stops the recording.

There's still nothing here that could put me in prison. But the duffel could be problematic.

There are two more files and I open each one to find the compromising photos Blue would have used to blackmail the other two before me. Unless there are files hidden within folders, and there may well be, I don't find anything else.

I close the laptop and set it aside. I'll give it to Robbie tomorrow. I turn my attention to her. Fire crackles in the grate behind her as I sip my whiskey. Well, Carlton's whiskey, but he doesn't need it where he is.

"You and I find ourselves in a predicament, don't we? A conundrum. I rarely get to use that word."

She shifts in her seat.

"See, I don't believe you're being wholly truthful with me."

"I answered all your questions."

"Not to mention my duffel bag allegedly stashed away in some locker in some bus terminal."

"I don't know what you want from me."

"I'm getting to that. You're not very patient. Tell me something. What was your plan if I paid you anyway?"

She shrugs a shoulder. "Get Wren. Go to Canada maybe."

"Did you call in the tip that got your father arrested?"

"How did you know about that?"

"I'll take that as a yes. You were going to take your sister to Canada so he wouldn't find either of you?"

She nods.

"That postcard, you went white when you saw it."

She clams up at that.

"Is it from him?"

Nothing.

"You're afraid he's going to come after you? Even though he's in prison."

"He has friends outside."

"The postcard is from him?" I repeat my question. She wrings her hands in her lap, and fear flashes in her eyes. She shifts her gaze away for a moment. I wait until she turns back to me and nods. "Tell me something else, how long do you think a-hundred-grand will last you when you're paying for your sister's medical care?"

"Look, what is this all about? You have me. And I'm guessing you figured out by now, like I have figured out, that I'm in over my head. So maybe you can just tell me what you want. You want to punish me? Fine. Do it. You're not going to kill me."

"No?"

She shakes her head. She's right, though.

"What the hell do you want exactly, Zeke?"

I smile, and I imagine for the outside, for what she sees, I am calm. Reasonable even.

Her gaze narrows. "Is it sex? You want to fuck me? Is that the arrangement?"

I snort.

"Don't laugh at me."

"But you're funny."

Her hands fist and she leaps to her feet. "Just fucking tell me so I can get it over with and get on with my life!"

"I didn't tell you to get up." She must see the change in my expression because she looks uncertain but then folds her arms across her chest and glares at me.

I swallow the last of my whiskey and stand. At that she takes a step backward but there's nowhere for her to go.

Closing the space between us, I stand over her and she has to crane her neck back to look at me, but I note the still stubborn jut of her jaw. She's not backing down.

The fire crackles at her back. I reach around to caress her hair.

"Naïve little Blue." I cradle her skull before weaving my fingers into her thick hair and making a fist.

She makes a sound and grabs my forearm as I haul her onto tiptoes. She sets her hands against my chest for balance as she stares up at me, big eyes betraying her panic. She's very pretty, and the fear that's coming off her, that I can fucking smell, fuck, it makes my dick hard.

"You think all I want is a fuck and you can simply get on with your life after you try to blackmail me? To destroy me?" I ask, walking her slowly toward the desk.

"You're hurting me." She struggles but she'll heel. She has no choice. She will learn that tonight.

"I already told you once, I'm a little more complicated than that." Once we reach the desk, I shift my grip to her throat and hug her back to my front.

She clutches my forearm, in a full panic as my fingers dig into the soft flesh of her neck, her pulse beating wildly beneath my thumb.

I dip my face down, inhale deeply at the crook of her neck before bringing my mouth to her ear and biting the lobe, tugging, hearing her whisper of breath as I press my erection against her ass.

"I smell you, Blue. I smell your fear. Tell me something, does it turn you on?" I tell her in a voice so low it's a whisper that makes her shudder. "Do you want me to fuck you? Is that it?"

"Let me go," she whispers desperately.

With a sweep of my arm, I clear the surface of the desk and push her down over it. Kicking her legs apart, I bunch her skirt up to her waist and smack her ass. She cries out, fingers closing around the edges of the desk, her back rigid when I grip the fleshiest part of that cheek and dig my fingers in.

"Not what you were expecting when you sent that first email, is it?" I ask.

"Zeke, I—"

I bend over her. "Ezekiel. I don't want to remind you again."

"Please. I—"

I straighten, look down at her bent over the desk, one of my hands splayed between her shoulder blades to keep her down, the other weighing that ass cheek. I squeeze, hear her yelp before I let go of her cheek to spank her again. She cries out as the sound of flesh meeting flesh reverberates around the room and my dick is so fucking hard, it's threatening to tear through my jeans. "Dangerous games have dangerous consequences, *Blue*. You're going to learn that lesson hard."

I slide the hand between her shoulder blades down to her lower back and press it into the desk, forcing her ass up, and I begin to rain down the spanking of her life.

13

BLUE

Zeke keeps me pinned as he spanks my ass and thighs, never letting up as I struggle, not once showing mercy when I beg for it. He alternates between cheeks and delivers smack after smack until I'm whimpering, my knees turned to mush. He's tireless and when I think I'll die if he spanks me just once more, he stops.

The only sounds in the room are the crackling of wood in the fire, my whimpering, ragged breaths, my begging, and Zeke's heavier breathing. I guess he exerted himself.

When the weight of his hand on my lower back lessens, I dare a glance, turning back over my shoulder to look at him. I'm expecting him to be gloating, a satisfied smirk on his face, but his eyes are dark, almost black, and locked on my ass.

His question repeats. Am I turned on? Do I want him to fuck me?

No. God. No. Of course not.

He blinks, shifts his gaze to meet mine and I swallow at the heat in his eyes.

"Stay," he commands. Those moth wings begin to flutter inside my stomach and I close my eyes and obey. When he places his hands on my throbbing ass and splays me open, I grip the edges of the desk.

Two knuckles slide over my soft, punished curves and I close my eyes, my breath ragged as his fingers slide over my sex. His touch is light at first, and I'm not even sure it's real or if I'm imagining it, but then fingers dip inside me and my breath shudders.

"Blue."

I swallow. Can he hear me swallow?

He presses his fingers deeper but the instant he feels me stiffen, he stops.

"Blue?" He probes, testing. Sweat breaks out over my forehead. Surely, he can't tell, can he? "Blue," he repeats.

Nothing. I can't move. Can't speak. Can't meet his gaze.

"Look at me."

I shake my head.

"Blue. Open your eyes and look at me."

It takes all I have but I do it, finally.

He holds my gaze, and he probes, and I'm up on tip toe, my legs stiff, every muscle tight. He tests my resistance, eyes confused? He cocks his head and pushes again and only stops when I let out a whimper.

His eyebrows furrow but he can't feel the barrier, can he? He makes a sound I can't quite decipher the meaning of. Only when he draws his fingers out can I breathe again. Am I relieved? I'm not sure. Because I feel the loss of the intrusion and I hear the sound of my own wetness. Which, why the fuck am I wet?

"Keep looking at me," he says, and I do. I swallow again, my breathing coming in pants as he slides his fingers up to my asshole. Just like that first night. Except he doesn't stop. He circles that tight opening, and I grip the sides of the desk so hard my nails must leave marks in the wood.

"Jesus. Please." I close my eyes.

"No, that won't do. I said look at me."

I do, feeling my face burn as his fingers circle the tight ring of my ass.

"I want to be certain you understand something," he says, voice hoarse.

He presses against the opening, and I almost climb on top of the desk in my effort to get away, but he closes his free hand over my hip and holds me in place, ass cheek splayed, and a moment later, I moan. I fucking moan as he pushes his finger inside me.

When I open my eyes again, because I'd closed them, he's watching me, patient, and there's that smirk as he finger-fucks my ass, making me groan when he adds a second finger and hooks me, forcing me up to the very tips of my toes as his other hand slides between my legs, fingers coming to my clit.

"Oh. God!" I push my forehead into the desk as he rubs my clit, working his fingers expertly and forcing a deep moan from my throat as my knees buckle and I come. I come harder than I've ever come on my own and

I hate myself a little for it when, once it's over, once he's finished, he leans over me, his breath hot against my ear, his cock hard against my ass, and whispers his words to me.

"I want to be certain you understand that I own you, Little Convict. You're mine."

14

EZEKIEL

Her body sags as soon as I step away, knees wobbling. She holds onto the edges of the desk as if her life depends on it and lays her cheek down, staying put when I step away.

What a good girl. A good, submissive, girl. This is exactly the result I wanted, although, honestly, I hadn't meant to finger-fuck her. Hadn't meant to make her come.

I take in the sight of her punished ass. The wetness smeared along her thighs. She's fully exposed to me. Mine.

Something inside my chest rumbles at that word.

Mine.

I like it. I want it.

She sniffles. She's trying not to cry or at least not let me see her cry. Doesn't she know yet I'll have her tears and her pain? They belong to me. She belongs to me.

"Straighten up," I finally say.

She moves slowly, like it takes all her energy to peel

her fingers from the desk. She reaches back, fingertips brushing her ass cheeks lightly. I'm sure it hurts. She smooths her skirt down to cover herself. I watch as she straightens. She's barefoot. She must have lost her shoes at some point.

She won't meet my eyes as she quickly wipes at hers. Her face burns red. It should. She was wet. She was wet from that spanking, and she came with my fingers in her ass. It's a good sign. I will enjoy making use of that hole as well as the others.

"Gather your skirt and hold it at your waist."

"What?"

"You heard me."

"You're an asshole," she says.

"Are we back to that?"

She glares but gathers up her skirt, her blush deepening as I openly drag my gaze to the slit of her shaved pussy.

Her virgin pussy.

I felt the barrier. At the thought, that rumbling comes from inside my chest. *Mine.* She hears it but she's not experienced enough to understand just what it means.

"Sit down on the stool."

She looks at it, then at me. That wood cannot be comfortable on an un-spanked ass. "I'm fine to stand."

"Sit anyway." I pour myself another whiskey and watch her ass as she crosses to that stool and perches on the edge of it, wincing. I'm sure it's nothing compared to my hand, I think, wondering if I should tell her to be grateful it was only my hand.

I resume my seat on the armchair and study her, smiling down at her.

"This is already so much better. Was it the spanking or coming on my fingers that seems to have humbled you?"

She grits her teeth, raises her stubborn chin. "I hate you."

I shrug a shoulder. "If only that were true. Now open your legs."

"No."

"I've already seen it all. Touched it all. I'll fuck it all soon, starting with your tight little asshole."

"Jesus." She's unable to hold my gaze, which makes this so much more enjoyable.

"So, I guess you're right in some way. I do plan to fuck you. But that's not all. Open your legs, Blue. Don't be shy."

Her eyes narrow and I imagine the curses she's hurling my way as she spreads her legs open.

"Here you go, *Zeke*." She waits for my reaction and one corner of her mouth curves upward. She sees my irritation at her inviting herself to use the shortened form of my name. Her gaze slowly dips down to my crotch. "You like what you see?"

"I do," I say, taking in how the slit yawns open to display the gleaming pink of her pussy. I bring my fingers to my nose and watch her flush red when I inhale deeply, her scent an aphrodisiac. I drink my whiskey, enjoying the sight for a long moment before dragging my gaze back to hers. "Tell me something, Blue. You never did say.

What is it you think I did exactly?" I ask, because as beautiful as her wet little cunt is, this is not about that.

A furrow forms between her brows at the change in topic. She bites her lip, small white teeth pressing against the swollen lower lip. I wonder if she realizes how enticing that is because I'm still hard and I'm going to need to take care of that soon. I should warn her. Hell, I'd have her suck me off if I was sure she wouldn't bite but we're not there yet and I won't fuck her until I'm sure she's clean and there's no risk of accidents. Although, if my guess is right, and she is a virgin, well, time will tell, and, opposite her, I'm patient.

"Blue?"

She looks away, considers something and I wonder if she's ever actually thought it through. If she's said the words to herself, much less out loud. Would she be so brazen if she had? If she truly understood what I did?

She looks at me. "The man in the car was your father. The woman wasn't your mother."

"Correct, go on. What did I do?"

"You tampered with the breaks or something."

I don't blink. Hearing it doesn't stir up any emotion, any guilt, any regret. I am unbothered. That *should* be worrying.

"Say it. Say what I did."

The room is so silent the only sound is the crackling of the fire, the flames, the occasional pop of damp wood. It doesn't matter that it's warm for a fire. I like it.

"Say it, Blue."

The pulse on her neck jumps. She licks her lips. "You

killed them. You killed your father and the woman he was with."

Does it make me a monster that my heartbeat remains level, that nothing shifts inside me to hear the words spoken aloud

I murdered my father. Patricide. Where are the Furies who should be taunting me? Driving me mad. Sending me to an early grave.

No such luck.

"Does it scare you to know I'm capable of such an act?"

She considers this for a long moment before she finally answers. And, on this night of nights, after all that's transpired between us, her answer is the thing that makes me stop. It is the single most surprising and stunning thing of all.

"No. Not all fathers protect their children. He must have done something terrible to you. And it gives me hope. Because I want to kill mine."

15

BLUE

There was one thing, one detail, I never told anyone. One secret I kept.

When I got home that day, when I went into the bathroom to find my father holding Wren's head under water, she was naked. And his pants were undone, open and pushed half-way down his ass. There was blood on the fronts of his thighs and his face was badly scratched.

"Go upstairs," Zeke says, and, for the first time since I've been in this house, I know I've rattled him. What I said, did I know it was true before? Did I know this was what I wanted before saying it out loud?

I wipe a stray tear. It's not for myself or for what I have to do. What I will do. It's for Wren. It's for the life she lost, because even if she's alive, she lost the life she should have had.

"Go to bed. Now," he says.

"My sister. Tomorrow, she'll—"

"I said go to bed, Blue."

"Promise me you'll take me to see her first. Promise me. Please."

He nods once but is no longer looking at me, so I get up, and I go upstairs, making my way to the same room as earlier and closing the door. I don't even care if he'll lock it. It doesn't matter. I strip off my clothes and without bothering to find anything to sleep in, I climb into the bed, exhausted, and crawl under the covers to sleep.

My mind wanders to what happened between us. No. Not between us. To what he did. Making me come like that. What he said. But I force the thoughts away and squeeze my eyes shut, trying to ignore the fluttering of wings in my belly, the memory of how it felt when I came.

When I open my eyes, it's to bright light shining on my face. I slept hard. I can't remember the last time I slept so hard.

I turn to the window, take in the warmth of the sun. Sunday. Wren's birthday. I sit up and nearly have a fucking heart attach when I find Zeke comfortably ensconced in the chair across the room watching me.

"Jesus!" I put my hand over my heart, half-up on one elbow. "Jesus fucking Christ!"

He studies me, eyes intent, and I'm not sure if he just got here or if he's been here all night.

"What the hell are you doing?" I ask, sitting up, careful to keep the duvet over myself. I note I'm not chained to the bed. That's positive, I guess.

He pushes a hand through his hair and blinks, then stands. I wonder where his mind was.

"Morning," he says.

"How long have you been in here?"

"A while," he says shamelessly. He walks toward the suitcase picking my discarded skirt and sweater up from the floor on his way. "You should take care of the clothes. They're on loan." He drapes last night's things neatly over the back of a chair and rifles through the suitcase to pick out a dress. He comes to the bed and lays it there. It's pretty. Midnight blue with a cinched waist and short, A-line skirt.

"It's a little cold for this maybe?" It's March and mornings and evenings are still cold, and the dress has short sleeves.

He digs around in the suitcase to find a sweater. He tosses that onto the bed as well.

"I'm taking you to visit your sister. Then you and I have an appointment."

I am relieved. One victory at a time. "I can be ready in ten minutes. But I need my makeup. It's in my purse."

"You don't need that."

"I do. People will stare—"

"Doesn't matter what people think."

"No. It's Wren… It upsets her."

At that he stops. "Does she have any memory of that night?"

"I… I hope not."

"Good. Get dressed. I'll see you downstairs." He walks toward the door.

"What appointment do we have after?"

He stops and turns back into the room. "Well, I was going to have you submit to a virginity test, but I don't think there's a need." He grins. Remembering last night, I feel my face burn and try to ignore the heat. "But I do need to be sure you're clean and that I'm protected."

"First, wow, okay, I'm not sure where to start with that gem. Not even certain if I heard right," I say flippantly, grateful he seems to be back to his asshole self and I won't have to think about what happened last night.

"You did."

"A virginity test? What the hell even is that?"

"Something you don't need to worry about as I've already established, you're a virgin. Which, honestly, is surprising in this day and age—"

"Fuck off."

He grins. "Women within The Society are required to remain virgins until marriage. The test is standard."

"Well, that's very modern of you."

"We're not a modern society."

"I'm not a part of your creepy little society."

"But you will play by my rules since you inserted yourself into my life."

I open my mouth to argue, close it again and shake my head. "Wait, so you want to be sure *I'm* clean and *you're* protected?" I ask, pointing from myself to him.

"Correct."

"What about me? I mean, out of the two of us, I think I'm the one who should be worried about picking up some STD, don't you? I mean, not that I've agreed to making love with you."

He snorts. "Just to be clear, we'll be fucking. There will be no love making."

"I didn't mean—" I start, embarrassed, but he cuts me off.

"Specifically, I'll be fucking you. I'll expect your submission."

Once again, I'm grateful he's such a prick. "You're quite the romantic," I say, trying again for flippant.

"I'm not going for romantic. That's part of the arrangement I mentioned last night. Before we got... off track."

He smirks.

I grit my teeth. "You offered your protection for the information I have."

"I guess I'm amending." He casually shrugs a shoulder. "Anyway, back to what I was saying, you're safe from me. For the moment." He steps toward the bed. I lean backward, tug the duvet higher because there's something in his eyes that makes my stomach feel like a thousand moths have taken flight. And he must see it. "But let's get clear on something. What you told me last night, what you want, it doesn't change anything, not for us. It just makes this a little more complicated. Now get dressed. We're on a schedule."

"I'm not—"

"I'm sure your sister would hate to miss your visit," he says, checking his watch as he walks to the door. "Get dressed."

"This conversation isn't over." He shrugs a shoulder and he's out in the hallway. "Wait! I need to stop at the apartment and pick up Wren's gift." He sighs. "I'll be quick. And it's on the way."

"That's up to you and how quickly you're up and we're out."

"You are such a jerk."

"Time waits for no man."

I flip him off, but he doesn't see it because he's long gone. I hurry to get dressed, brush my teeth and wash my face, finger combing my hair. It's wavy and falls into place fairly easily, especially short as it is. I head downstairs and hear Zeke talking to a woman and I see Cynthia, the cook from last night, in the kitchen. She smiles at me when she sees me.

"Good morning," I say, trying to be friendly. "Whatever you're making smells wonderful."

"Morning," she says with a smile, although I see how her eyes dip to the chain hanging off the collar still around my neck. I casually wrap my hand around my throat to hide it. "I'm making omelets. Any dietary restrictions?"

I look at Zeke, who is drinking coffee, then turn back to Cynthia. "I eat everything. Thanks, Cynthia. I'm Blue, by the way." She smiles again. "Aren't you eating?" I ask Zeke.

"I've been up for a while."

"Watching me sleep," I mutter under my breath. "My purse?"

He points and I don't know how I missed it sitting on the counter along the back wall. I pick it up, rummaging through for my makeup.

"There's a bathroom down the hall you can use," he says, watching me differently than he was before. Like he's trying to figure me out.

I walk to the bathroom, taking in the house, noticing the dust cloths are off most of the furniture and light pours in from the oversized windows. The house is beautiful, and I imagine cost a fortune to furnish. I wonder about the electricity bill then remember he said it's not his house. I wonder whose it is.

On my way to the bathroom, I pass the study. The things that were on the desk are still lying on the floor and I look quickly away remembering what he did. I touch my ass, which is still sore from the spanking which, followed by, well, by what followed, was the least of my humiliations.

That takes me to what he said earlier. A virginity test? What the fuck? And testing that I'm clean. What about him? I'm sure out of the two of us he's the one to worry about. I get it he wants to fuck me. Why not? I'm under his control and he's not made a secret of finding me attractive. Even if he didn't, he's a man and men will fuck anything, right? So truly, why not? I'd be different than any woman he'd date. No hassle. And no choices. When he says bend over, I'll be bending over.

My body's reaction to it all, though, isn't what it should be. I shouldn't be attracted to him. I shouldn't want him to touch me.

With a groan, I force the thoughts out of my mind and walk into the bathroom. I switch on the light. It, like the rest of the house, is bright and beautiful with its pedestal sink made completely of marble, antique brass fixtures and mirror. I don't dally, though. I hurry to put on my makeup. What takes the most time is the foundation because I have to layer and blend so well. I meant what I said. It upsets Wren to see it. But I also don't like anyone staring and they do stare.

He asked if she remembered that night and I hope

she never does. Let that be the one blessing of what happened to her. The damage he did.

Ten minutes later, I return to the kitchen to find Cynthia plating an omelet for me. There's also juice and coffee. Zeke's gone. I drink the juice first and eat the omelet. I'm starving, again. I feel like I've been starving for years.

I'm almost finished my plate when he returns carrying the laptop and the Ziploc containing the gun.

"You ate all that?" he asks, looking surprised.

"I don't waste food," I say, wiping the corner of my mouth. I'm sure a man like him has never known hunger, so I don't bother to explain myself.

He looks at my face and I'm suddenly self-conscious.

"It's fine," he says. "You can't see it."

I nod, turn to Cynthia. "Thanks for breakfast. That was really good. Are you getting rid of the bacon?" I ask, seeing the extra strips in the pan that she's carrying toward the sink.

"Unless you want them," she says, eyebrows raised.

I walk over, pick them out of the pan and eat them, too. "What?" I ask Zeke who is staring at me.

"Nothing. Wash your hands. I don't want grease in my car."

I roll my eyes and wash my hands, remembering the first night I was here. Has it only been forty-eight hours?

"Let's go," Zeke says and gestures to the front door.

"What are you doing with those?" I ask about the things he's holding.

"Dropping them off with my brother. I know someone who's good with computers." His expression is mocking.

"Oh. There's nothing on there."

"Well, then you won't mind if I just make sure for myself," he says and opens the front door.

"One more thing," I say, turning to face him. I pull the chain up from under my dress. "Wren won't understand what this is."

He grins. "You can explain it to her. Or I can."

I shake my head. "This is serious. Take it off."

"When are you going to learn you don't call the shots."

"Please take it off," I force myself to say. "Just until our visit is over. You can put it right back on after."

He sighs. "I'm not heartless." He sets the laptop and the Ziplock down on the table beside the door and takes a small key out of his pocket. "Look up."

I do. He steps closer, close enough that I can smell his aftershave. He bends down, and I try not think about how I smell hints of leather in his aftershave or feel anything like that ridiculous shudder as his fingertips brush the skin at my throat while he unlocks the delicate but strong chain.

He straightens, eyes locked on me as he slowly pulls it up out of my dress, taking his time as he gathers it up in the palm of one big hand.

"Just keep in mind I did that for you without asking anything in return," he says, pocketing chain and key.

"You're so generous."

He raises an eyebrow, and I think he's amused. But no, that can't be right. Is a man like him ever amused?

I blink away and turn to step out into the sunshine where an SUV is parked on the circular drive. He passes me to unlock the door and opens the passenger side, but before I step in, he wraps a hand around the back of my neck, stopping me.

Does he feel that subtle spark of electricity? Does my skin burn his like his does mine? What is it about this man that has me feeling these strange, unfamiliar feelings? I should hate him. At the very least be afraid of him, and in some ways, I am, but there's something else too. Him offering his protection in exchange for information and my sexual submission, I don't know, I should rebel at least against that last part, but that's not what I want to do. I want it. I want all of it.

And out of all of that, I'm stuck on one word: protection.

To be protected. To feel protected.

I haven't felt protected in a long, long time. I've felt hunted.

And out of anyone I have ever known, even my own mother who did the best she could, I feel like if anyone can protect me, if anyone can keep me safe, it's Zeke.

I try to make my face blank as I look up at him. He can't know what I'm thinking. He'll just use it against me. Mock me.

He's got to be a foot taller than me and, as if to make sure I get the message, he gives my neck a squeeze to show me he's also much stronger than me. I didn't need the reminder.

"Why did you tell me that?" he asks.

"Why did I tell you what?"

"About your father."

I squint up into the sunshine, shrug a shoulder. "I don't know."

"You don't know why you told me, or you didn't know you wanted that?"

Perceptive, this man. I need to be careful. "Don't know," I lie.

"You do. Just to be clear, nothing has changed between us. What I told you last night, it stands. What I'm doing now I'm doing for your sister. Considering what happened to her. You do anything stupid today, and I'll punish you. And it won't be a simple spanking. Clear?"

"And you'll enjoy every moment of my punishment, I'm sure."

One corner of his mouth curves upward into a grin. "On second thought, do something stupid."

I roll my eyes and tug free of him to climb into the car.

16

EZEKIEL

The heat of her skin scorches my hand. I don't miss her shudder at my touch. I don't miss how she licks her lips when she looks up at me, even if she's unaware of it herself. I still very clearly remember how her body reacted to me last night.

What she said at the end of the night I still have to unpack.

She climbs into the passenger seat of the SUV. I set the laptop in the backseat then lean over her to strap her in. Her breath catches for the second time in just a few minutes and her nipples tighten, pressing against the fabric of her dress.

Last night, after I sent her to bed, I remained in the study until the fire died down and drank Carlton Bishop's whiskey. I then went upstairs to her room. Maybe I slept in that chair for a few minutes now and again. Maybe it was jet lag. But I watched her. I don't know why exactly. It's a creepy move, I know, but I had to.

I search her eyes. Why did what she said have such an

impact on me? I don't care about her. She's no one to me. Is it guilt? Or a twisted chance at redemption? There is no redemption for me. No atonement for my sin, because it cost Zoë her life. So, what is it about Blue that has me unable to look away? To walk away? What is it that holds me here, invested, because I am. And it has nothing to do with what she knows about me.

I study her face, watch the pink creeping up her neck as her eyes dart just beyond my shoulder. We're at eye-level with her in the high SUV. I touch her jaw, turn her face to mine. She licks her lips yet again. She's very pretty and when the blue of her eyes deepens, I know it's her body's reaction to my touch. She wants me to touch her as much as I want it. I try to read beyond the desire in her eyes, to the darkness just beyond. I want to understand the woman who spoke words of patricide the night before. The woman who is somehow not afraid to be with a man she knows murdered his own father.

I don't know what it is, why it is that I've taken such an interest in Blue Thorne. Maybe it's because of Zoë. Because I failed her so wholly that I'm hyper aware now, with Blue. I don't know. I should try to remember why she's here. Pretty as she is, she's an extortionist. I should keep it in mind, even though there's another side to this. Her motivation is not greed. She will do whatever she needs to do to look after her sister. Selfless as her quest may be, though, it should not cloud my judgment. What she wants cannot become my problem.

I don't know what she sees in my eyes but she's unable to hold my gaze. She turns her head, pushes her hand through the waves of blue and black hair.

I close her door, glad to have that barrier between us as the thought of her in my bed wakes a thing inside me that should be left to lie. My sister was broken physically, emotionally, mentally, by the end. Me, physically, I am whole. Emotionally, I'm a corpse. And yet, it's my mind that worries me because it is a twisted, dark thing. And there is a part of me that knows that for Blue to be safe, she needs to stay out of it.

When I came back to New Orleans not forty-eight hours ago, it was with the intention of confronting my blackmailer, taking care of the situation however I needed to take care of it. Now, it's all changed. Nothing has gone as I expected. I should be on a flight back to Amsterdam. To the half-life I'm living there. But here I am taking my blackmailer to visit her broken sister.

With a shake of my head, I climb into driver's side and start the engine. Before I've put the SUV into drive, my phone alerts me to a message. I glance at the text. It's from Robbie.

Robbie: Lucky Tommy just made parole. He'll be out in a week. Someone pulled some strings.

Me: Any idea who?

Robbie: Not yet.

I glance at Blue who is chewing on her lip.

She shifts her gaze to me. "Does this car drive itself? If you're busy sexting your girlfriend, I can drive."

"No girlfriend."

"Shocker." She turns her attention to peeling the last of the old polish from a fingernail.

I shift my attention to my phone.

Me: Did the hospital run any other tests on Wren or Blue?

Robbie: Be more specific.

Me: Rape

Robbie: I'll dig to see what I can find. Should be landing in about an hour.

Me: I'll see you tonight then. I'm dropping off a laptop and a gun at Jericho's.

He sends an emoji with eyebrows raised high. I ignore it. I slip the phone into my pocket and drive. When I should turn right onto the road that will take us to Blue's apartment, though, I turn left.

"It's the other way," Blue says.

"I know."

She watches me, distrustful, as we drive down the short street that leads to the tall gates that open at our approach. I pull through, very aware of how rigid Blue's spine is, how she's watching, one eye on those gates in the mirror as they close behind us. I could ease her mind. If I were good, maybe I would, but I don't say a word.

Once we get to the entrance of the St. James house, the front door opens, and my brother steps out.

Blue glances at me. "Stay," I tell her, killing the engine and pocketing the key before I reach back for the laptop and Ziploc. I don't close the driver's side door and Jericho peers into the vehicle as I approach.

"What's this?" he asks, gesturing toward Blue.

I hand him the things. "It's her sister's birthday."

His eyebrows shoot up. "What the fuck are you doing, Zeke?" he asks after a beat.

"Leverage. That's all."

"You sure about that?"

"Password is FuckthePatriarchy. Capital F and P. No

spaces. Robbie's flight is landing in about an hour. He'll come directly here."

"And the gun?"

"Found it at her place. We should see if we can figure out who it's registered to. If it's registered, that is." I check my watch. "I have to go."

He puts a hand on my shoulder. "Brother. I ask you again. What the hell are you doing?" When I don't have an answer for him, he sighs. "If this has to do with Zoë, you know—"

"Too late to have anything to do with Zoë, don't you think?" I shrug off his hand.

"Zeke, I—"

"I need to go."

When I turn back to the SUV, I wish I'd closed the door because from the look on Blue's face, I know she heard every word of that exchange. I get in and slam the door shut. I drive, feeling her gaze bore into the side of my head.

"You and your brother seem close," she taunts.

"Shut up, Blue."

"No, really, I got the warm fuzzies seeing you two together."

I shoot her a warning look. "Shut. Up."

"Who's Zoë? Sounded like a sore spot—"

I slam on the brakes just as we exit the gates and Blue jerks forward, yelping, gripping the dashboard as the seatbelt digs into her chest. At exactly the same moment I fling my arm out, my hand closing around her throat. It's not even a conscious thought. It just happens.

"When I tell you to shut up, I mean it. You have no

idea what you're talking about," I spit the words, any composure is gone, my rage on full display.

Her hands wrap around my forearm, fingernails digging into skin as I squeeze her neck, watching how her eyes tear up. She makes a sound, a croaked plea, and a tear slides over her cheek. I watch it, hypnotized by its slow descent. Her nails break skin and I welcome the pain. It takes a moment before I meet her terrified gaze and force a deep breath in. It takes all I have to ease my grip, to release her. She exhales, clutches her throat and I find my thumb coming to that tear, smearing it, unable to look away.

She shudders, sucking in air, back of her head pressed firmly into the headrest.

More tears fall from her eyes, the whites, pink, making the blue even prettier somehow, and I watch her. I lose myself for a moment in the depths of those eyes. It seems it's all I can do.

"You're very pretty when you cry." I don't recognize my own voice, but I do hear how that sounds.

"You're sick, you know that?" she mutters, wiping away the steadily streaming tears. "You're fucking sick."

"You have no idea." I draw back, ease my foot off the brake.

17

BLUE

I don't know what the fuck that was in the SUV. Zoë is a sore spot and his relationship with his brother is fucked up, but those things aren't my problem. I need to focus.

"I'll be quick," I say once we get to the apartment and Zeke parks. I open the passenger side door and climb out.

"I don't think so," Zeke says. He's out of the SUV before I can slip away, taking hold of my arm as I try to scoot past him. We walk into the apartment building.

"I'm not going to run. I can't without leaving my sister behind and I won't do that," I say as we walk up the stairs, his hand tight around my arm. He doesn't comment as we climb the stairs to my floor. "Christ, are you trying to break my arm?" I ask when we get to the door. He must realize how tightly he's holding on to me and releases me to dig my keys out of his pocket.

He unlocks the apartment door and opens it. It's exactly as I'd left it, all the furniture that isn't mine that will be here for the next tenant after I'm gone.

"Get what you need," he says, checking the time.

I walk into the apartment and head toward the bedroom, Zeke following me. There's just a couple of things I need. One is the photo of Mom, Wren and me. It's the only photo I have of Mom. I pick it up, smile when I look at it. The memory is sweet, but looking at it now is bitter. They're both gone, even Wren, because who she was is no longer.

I take an old tote hanging on the closet door and put the photo inside, then reach for a shoebox on the top shelf. I can't quite manage to get to it, but Zeke extends an arm and easily lifts the box out and sets it on the bed for me. "Thanks," I say, opening the lid and shuffling through what is mostly junk. Buried beneath it all is a small, black velvet bag. Inside that is a necklace. It's our mom's. She never took it off. It's a medal of the Virgin Mary. It was on the nightstand the day she disappeared. It's how I know she didn't just leave. Well, it's one of the ways I know. First thing she did every morning was put it on and say a little prayer.

"Is that it?" he asks.

"Almost."

His phone rings and I'm grateful when he steps away. I hurry to grab a pile of underthings and a pair of jeans and shove them, too, into the tote. Without waiting for permission, I slip into the bathroom. "I just need to use the bathroom real quick," I say as I lock the door. I hurry to pull on a pair of panties and, after taking a deep breath in, I flush the toilet, then lift the lid of the tank, hoping the flushing of the toilet will cover any sound of what I'm doing. I feel under the rim and find what I'm looking for.

What I'd hidden. My fingers come into contact with the small Ziploc bag. I peel the tape off and look at it. This is one thing I learned from my dad. Never leave all your eggs in one basket. The go bag was one thing. If anyone ever found it, took the cash, Wren and I would be screwed. So, there's a second stash of cash. Another two grand. And along with it, a small flash drive.

My father's laptop is empty because I emptied it. All of his files are on the thumb drive.

A knock on the door startles me. "Blue? What are you doing?"

I hurry to shove the roll of cash and flash drive into my pocket and replace the lid.

"What people do in bathrooms," I call out, running the water as I tell myself to relax so I sound natural.

"Open the door. Now." He bangs on it.

I unlock the door and open it. He has his fist raised to pound again.

"Whoa. I needed to change my tampon." I say which is not quite true although I do have my period. "Is that okay, or did you want to watch me do that, too?"

He looks at me and my heart is pounding. I'm not sure he believes me.

"Let's go," he finally says and gestures for me to go ahead of him. I do, relieved and we walk out of the building and to the SUV and head to Oakwood to see Wren.

18

EZEKIEL

B lue annoyingly flips radio channels the whole drive to the facility housing Wren. I'm not sure why I let her, but she must know a snippet of every song ever made because she can sing along to most. She's restless.

We arrive and I park the SUV, noticing how few cars are in the lot.

"It might be better if you just wait here," she says.

"Nah. I'd love to meet your sister."

"She might get upset."

"You're not going in alone, Blue."

"Fine. I just need to stop by the gift shop," she says and strolls ahead of me.

"Why? You have a gift."

"She likes balloons. And teddy bears," she says. We walk into the building. The gift shop is just by the entrance. Blue chooses the biggest bouquet of Happy Birthday balloons and a huge purple teddy bear. We get to the register. The woman rings up her items, making small talk, and when she tells us the cost, Blue looks up at me, eyebrows high, expectantly looking at me. "Pay the lady," she says, the smile on her face telling me how pleased she is with herself.

"Christ." I take out my wallet.

"Wait. Those flowers too. She'll love those," Blue says.

I reach over her and tap my card to the reader, tucking it back into my wallet before taking hold of her by the back of her neck. She gathers up the purchases, shoving the flowers into my hand.

"Their prices are extortion," I comment.

"It's all for a good cause. Besides, it's what money's for. To be spent," she taunts.

"My money, you mean."

"You confiscated my wallet and phone. I had no means to pay."

"It's all right. You can pay me back later. In flesh," I tell her, squeezing her neck as I guide her to the front desk, appreciating her shocked expression. I'm enjoying sparring with Blue.

"Hi Marjorie," Blue says and signs in. I notice she uses Masterson.

"Hi Blue, how are you doing, hon?"

She puts the pen down and looks at the woman. "I'm doing just fine. How is Wren?"

"Excited about your visit."

Blue smiles at this but underneath it all, I glimpse sadness in her eyes. "I'm glad. Oh, um, this is my... boyfriend. Ezekiel."

Boyfriend? I raise my eyebrows at Blue.

"But you can call him Zeke. We all do, isn't that right, Zeke?"

I glare.

She grins.

"This is Marjorie," she says.

Marjorie waggles her eyebrows at Blue then turns to me. "Nice to meet you, Zeke."

I grunt.

"You'll have to excuse him. He doesn't have great social skills," she whispers loudly to Marjorie. "Very bad at taking cues too. Men." She shakes her head. "Am I right?"

Marjorie nods and Blue and I make our way down a hallway.

"You have your little fun with that?"

"I did."

"Am I your *boyfriend*?"

"How did you want me to introduce you, as my kidnapper?"

"I think you might have done a little better."

"Sorry if you're offended. You can also just wait for me in the car."

"Not a chance," I say. "And I told you, only my friends and family call me Zeke."

"You have friends?"

I lean in close. "We'll see how funny you can be when you're taking my cock up your—"

"Here we are!" Blue announces as a couple of nurses pass us, their faces shocked because they clearly overheard what I said.

I wink at one of the women as they walk past and turn

to take in Blue's beet-red face. I walk her backward toward the wall.

"Just trying to act the part of your boyfriend. Too much?"

"Jackass."

"I'm impressed. You're branching out from asshole."

She flips me off and turns to the door. "I don't know how she'll be so please be nice to her. Just try not to be yourself."

"I'm offended."

"Right." Blue pushes the door open and the moment we're inside, Wren spins and runs toward us.

"Blue!"

I watch Blue closely, see that crease between her eyebrows, watch how her eyes grow sadder. With effort, she forces her lips to stretch into a smile. She opens her arms to hug her sister. Wren is a couple of inches taller than Blue, and, although Blue is maybe a-hundred-ten-pounds soaking wet, Wren is so skinny, the skin around her collarbones is sunken and she has shadows like bruises under her eyes.

"Happy Birthday!" Blue says as Wren pulls away, eyes excitedly moving to the balloons floating over Blue's head.

"I love balloons!" Wren takes them from Blue. Blue holds the teddy bear out to her. Wren is over the moon and takes it, too, hugging it to herself like a small child would. "I love her!" she exclaims, and when she squeezes her eyes shut to squeeze the bear, Blue glances at me and when I notice how damp her eyes are, how she's trying very hard not to cry, she quickly turns away.

"Hi Rudy," Blue says, moving toward the male nurse. He's in his early twenties I'd guess and a big guy. He smiles warmly, enveloping Blue in a bear hug. Blue rests her cheek against his chest and closes her eyes. I watch her relax into him and something tightens in my gut.

She trusts him.

"Hey you," Rudy says.

After a long moment, I clear my throat and they all turn to me.

"Happy Birthday, Wren," I say, stepping toward Blue's sister, offering her a genuine smile.

Her smile falters and she stares up at me, uncertain. She takes a step backward, still hugging that bear to herself.

"Blue?" she asks, eyes on me.

Blue comes to my side. "This is Zeke, Wren. He drove me over here. And he got you these." She points to the flowers I'm holding. "Didn't you, Zeke?" I shift my gaze to Blue and see her serious expression. "Didn't you?" she asks again.

I hold the flowers out to Wren, feeling exactly like the asshole Blue accuses me of being, realizing why Blue grabbed those at the last minute. "Your sister said you like flowers as much as you do balloons," I say to Wren.

"He's okay," Blue whispers to Wren, squeezing her hand. "It's okay, Wren. He's not scary."

Aren't I though? I shouldn't be here.

"Would you look at those," Rudy says, stepping forward to take the flowers as Wren watches me, still wary. It makes me wonder what she remembers of the night that changed her life. If she's instinctively terrified of men now. Rudy looks like a big teddy bear. He exudes warmth and kindness. Me? Well, I am a different story. "What do you say, Wren?"

"Thank you," she says, sounding like a child made to do something they don't want to do. I feel uncomfortable under Wren's scrutinizing gaze, and, weirdly, want her to trust me. "Where's the cake?" Wren asks, turning to Rudy, her forehead furrowed. She then looks to Blue. "Blue, did you forget the cake?"

"Oh. Um, I—"

"It's in the car. I'll go get it," I say, remembering the café across from the gift shop on our way in. I hope they have cake. Blue looks up at me, surprised. "Be right back," I say.

"I'll go see if I can wrangle up a vase for these," Rudy says, and we step out of the room together. Once the door is closed, Rudy looks up at me.

"They'll have cupcakes in the café. Grab the rainbow ones," he says. "She'll like those. And I'll get some candles at the nurse's station."

"Thanks," I say, and we head in different directions. I buy all the cupcakes the café has so she will have her pick and when I return to Wren's room, Rudy is already back and he's arranging the flowers in the vase with Wren.

Blue looks at the box of colorful cakes then up at me. She nods once in approval and, for reasons I can't explain, I'm glad to have it.

"I hope you like cupcakes," I announce and Wren and Rudy both turn. When Wren sees the arrangement of colorful cakes, her face lights up and she walks over, mouth open in a surprised O.

"I'm going to have this one and this one and this one," she starts, pointing to the various cupcakes.

Blue walks over and takes the box from me. "Are you going to leave any for us?" she asks and Wren laughs, and, before she turns to follow her sister, looks up at me, that wary expression a little less so.

19

BLUE

An hour later, I climb into the passenger seat of the SUV and wave to my sister who is watching from the window of her room as we drive out of the lot. The necklace glints in the sun but I'm not sure she recognized it as being Mom's.

"Thanks for getting the cupcakes," I say, watching straight ahead once she's out of sight. "That was actually nice."

He nods, his eyebrows furrowed, his attention on merging with traffic.

"She was going to go to medical school. She'd been accepted." I'm looking straight ahead but see him glance at me from the corner of my eye. "God. I hate this so much," I say, pressing the heels of my hands into my eyes to stop myself from crying.

"Why didn't you tell the police it was your father?"

"I was afraid he'd hurt her worse."

"Not if he was in jail."

"I couldn't be sure he would be." I turn to him. "I was

sixteen at the time and my big sister suddenly wasn't the sister I knew. Mom was gone. I thought they'd separate us. Take me away from her since I was a minor. God knows where they'd put Wren."

"Is she afraid of all men or is it just me?"

I study him. He almost sounds like he cares but I know he doesn't.

He raises his eyebrows, waiting for my response.

"I'm going to tell you something that may be new to you, Zeke," I say, putting a hand on his arm. I'm not sure who is more surprised, him or me, but I pull it away quickly. "And I realize this may come as a shock to you, but you don't exactly give off the warm fuzzies."

He gives me a withering sideways glance.

I put my feet up on the seat and hug my knees. "But yeah, pretty much all men with the exception of Rudy."

"Take your shoes off if you're going to put your feet on the leather."

I raise my eyebrows and look at him. I cock my head. "Worried I'll dirty your car?" I ask, not moving my feet. Digging them in. "Does it bother you?"

He looks at me. "It's a nice car." With one quick motion, he knocks my feet off the seat.

"Fine. Anal much?"

"Yeah, actually." We fall into silence. "Your mother, what happened to her? She left?"

"She would never have left us. Never."

He glances at me momentarily. "Your father hurt her?"

I turn to look out the side window and shrug my

shoulders. "Don't know. All I know is she wouldn't have left us."

We drive for ten more minutes in silence.

"Why are you helping me?" I ask.

"How am I helping you?"

"This. Today. Bringing me to my sister. The cupcakes. The gifts—"

"You didn't give me a choice on the gifts."

"You didn't have to do any of it. You could literally lock me up in that giant house of yours and no one would be the wiser."

"It's not my house."

"That's not the point. You know what I mean."

He's quiet for a long moment and doesn't speak until we pull onto a long drive, and he kills the engine. He takes the keys out of the ignition and turns to me, expression, as ever, unreadable.

"I'm not scary, remember? Hell, maybe I'm just a nice guy," he deadpans.

I roll my eyes and turn toward the house, remembering what he'd said about our appointment.

"I don't think you're a nice guy," I tell him.

"No, you're right, I'm not. I'm not helping you, Blue. I'm helping myself. You threatened me. You threatened my family. You and I are enemies. Nothing has changed between us. Knowing Wren, well, she's another means to an end—"

"She's not a means to an end. She's a human being."

"You love her which makes her a vulnerability. Something I can and will use to make you heel."

I shake my head. "Of course you will," I say and turn away.

He takes my chin between thumb and forefinger and makes me look at him. "Don't get the wrong idea, sweetheart. What you said back there? I'm not your boyfriend."

I jerk my face out of his grasp. "I didn't think you were."

"And more importantly, you don't want me to be." Something in how he says it makes me pause. Sends an icy thrill down my spine. His eyes narrow and he reaches into his pocket to retrieve my chain. "Almost forgot."

I don't speak. Instead, I just tilt my head back, my heart pounding as he hooks the chain back in place on my collar, reaffirming our roles.

"That's better," he says. "It'll help you remember your place."

"I was just thanking you. That's all."

"Don't."

The front door of the house opens, and a man steps out in a white doctor's coat. Nausea makes the cupcake I ate sit like a brick in my belly.

"Let's go get this taken care of so I can deliver that punishment I promised last night."

Dr. Shore pretty much ignores me and talks to Zeke as I follow behind them. This must be his home office. There's a waiting area, which is empty, and beyond it is his large, very cold looking office.

A nurse is unfolding the stirrups from an examination table, and the soft hum that precedes the ringing in my ears begins. I stop, turn, walk straight into Zeke's chest. He catches me when I bounce off, holding onto my arms either because he knows I'm about to bolt or to steady me. Probably the former.

I close my eyes momentarily, taking a deep breath in and telling myself to calm down. The conscious breathing sometimes helps and I'm grateful now is one of those times. I look up at him, feeling flushed. When I realize my hands are pressed to his chest, I pull them away, get myself out of his grasp and step backward.

The nurse clears her throat and I glance at her. "Ms. Masterson, you can get undressed behind the curtain."

I turn back to Zeke. Look past him to the door.

"Don't be stupid," he warns.

"What about you?" I ask in a hissed whisper.

"What about me?"

"Do I get a confirmation that you're not carrying any STDs?"

He grins. "You get my word."

"And that has to be good enough?"

He nods. It's infuriating. "Go get undressed. You're wasting the doctor's time."

"Fine." I get up on tiptoe so only he can hear me. "You're an asshole," I tell him then turn and walk behind the divider. I hear them talk on the other side and take off my clothes, suddenly unsure what I'm supposed to do with that stupid chain. I can't hide it, not if I'm freaking naked. I slip on the robe that's hanging on a hook, confirm the flash drive and roll of money are secure in the pocket of my dress and step around to find the nurse waiting.

Zeke is having a conversation with the doctor. When he glances my way, I give him a hateful look.

"I'll hold onto your robe," the nurse says. I slip it off and hand it to her, not meeting her eyes. "Climb on up."

I do. I've never had an exam like this before. I just keep my eyes on the ceiling as the nurse moves my feet onto the stirrups and try not to think about the fact that I'm spread wide open. Wholly exposed. At least no one comments on the chain.

The doctor turns toward me, rolling a low stool ahead of himself. I don't want to look at Zeke but when I turn my head, I see how stiffly he's standing, his hands fists at his sides.

"We'll just get started with an exam," the doctor starts as my gaze moves to Zeke's face. His eyes meet mine just as a tear slips out of the inside corner of one eye. It slides over the bridge of my nose before it drops off.

I hate him. I hate Ezekiel St. James. I just hope he knows that.

"Let the nurse take the sample," he says suddenly.

The doctor, who is just about to take a seat on the stool between my legs, stops. "Excuse me?" he asks, turning to Zeke.

Curious, I watch Zeke who is no longer looking at me.

"Let the nurse take the sample. I have a few questions for you," he says.

"I can take all your questions once I've performed the exam—"

"I said let her do it."

Dr. Shore is clearly surprised, but he bites back whatever comment he was about to make and nods.

I'm as surprised. This lesson in humiliation, has he abandoned it?

Zeke crosses the room and opens the door. "Let's talk outside."

"Of course," the doctor says and a moment later they're both gone.

"Well, that is unusual," the nurse says before taking the doctor's place.

"What do you mean?"

"The Society men, well, they're a different breed.

Often there are witnesses... well, I shouldn't gossip. I'm sure Dr. Shore won't like that. Now, let's get this done and you can relax."

"I have my period. It's light, but..." I trail off.

"That's no problem."

I turn to the door and although the exam is uncomfortable, it's not terrible and it's over quickly. Once she's finished with the exam, she administers a birth control shot which I don't argue against. I don't want to get pregnant any more than Zeke wants. After that, it's over and I move behind the screen to get dressed emerging just as the office door opens. I meet Zeke's gaze. His brow is furrowed, and I wonder if he's as confused as I am about what he just did.

"Let's go," he says once the nurse explains that they'll call him with the results.

I don't thank anyone. I slip past Zeke and hurry through the house and outside. I don't need to look over my shoulder to know he's right there. Using the key fob, he unlocks the door just as I reach it and I quickly step into the passenger side. His phone rings and he pauses before entering the driver's side. I watch him and wish I could hear what he was saying because the way he's looking at me, I know it's about me.

He finally nods and ends the call, tucking the phone into his pocket before climbing into the SUV. He starts the engine and sets it into Drive.

"Why did you do that?" I finally ask once we're on the road.

"Do what?"

"Have the nurse examine me."

He doesn't even glance at me. "I had questions for the doctor."

"I don't believe you."

He snorts, this time he looks at me. "What's your theory then?"

"You saw I was uncomfortable."

"And I took pity on you?"

I shrug a shoulder, suddenly feeling stupid for having brought it up.

He chuckles. I notice his gaze keeps moving to the rear-view mirror. It makes me anxious but when I look back, nothing stands out.

"Where are we going?" I ask when I notice that instead of going back to the house, he drives toward the French Quarter.

"Dinner," he says, checking his rear-view mirror yet again before turning off the main road.

"You're taking me out to dinner?"

He glances at me. "It's not a date, don't worry." He takes another turn.

I shrug a shoulder and sit back. That's fine. If he wants to feed me, he can go ahead. I can always eat.

I've gotten to know New Orleans pretty well and I notice he's taking a strange route that keeps us parallel along smaller streets rather than taking the straight shot into town. It'll take twice as long this way and I'm curious why he's doing it. I watch him, see his eyes move to the rear-view mirror again.

"Are you looking for something?" I ask.

"A parking spot. Ah." He parallel parks with ease in

front of an exclusive restaurant in a boutique hotel. I've seen it mentioned for their exceptional steak in various magazines I've perused while on my breaks at The Cat House. A line of cabs stands waiting across the street.

He puts the SUV into Park and glances once more in his rear-view mirror, then at the car that passes us. It's a black Audi and something about it startles me. My heart pounds because I swear, I recognize it. But it can't be. There's no way.

"Blue?" The car slows at the crosswalk as a mother crosses the street alongside her young child on a bike. I turn to find Zeke watching me.

"Yeah?"

"Ready?"

"For what?" No. I'm mistaken. There are probably thousands of black Audis in New Orleans. I don't even know the model. Do they all have rosary beads hanging from the rear-view mirror though?

"Dinner." His gaze follows mine to the car which is pulling away from the crosswalk. "See someone you know?" he asks, too perceptive.

I shake my head maybe too quickly because his eyes narrow infinitesimally.

"Let's go in," he finally says once it disappears from view.

"Yeah, okay." I look up at the restaurant. This is good. Dinner is good. Because whether or not I recognize the car, it just goes to show I'm not safe. Wren isn't safe. My father knows where we are, and he's not the only person looking for me. There's the man who hired him, for starters, who came looking for the laptop after his arrest.

If my father could find me from behind bars, then that man with more means could easily do so, too. The longer Wren and I are in New Orleans, the more dangerous this becomes.

Once we're back in the house, I'm trapped. There's no way I can get away. Here, maybe I can pretend to use the bathroom, slip out. I eye all those waiting taxis. There's a chance at least.

But am I safer with him? Can he truly protect me? He doesn't know the whole story. He only knows about my father. And what about Wren? She can't protect herself at all.

No. I need to get away from Ezekiel St. James, get Wren and get out of town. And this may be my only chance.

"I'm starving, actually. Thanks."

He gets out of the car and comes to my side to open my door. I climb out, clear my throat and tug my sweater closer. I take my tote with me.

He gestures to the entrance and when we reach it, a uniformed attendant opens the door. Soft piano music plays inside, the lighting a gentle, golden glow and tables set with sweeping white tablecloths and more silverware than I know what to do with.

The hostess glances at me, her resting bitch face firmly in place. When she looks up at Zeke, she rearranges her features, smiling wide, blinking what must be ten pounds of fake eyelashes at him. I want to roll my eyes.

"Table for two. Something private."

"Do you have a reservation, Mr..." she trails off.

He gives her a smile. "No, but I'm sure you can find room for us." He peers at her nametag. "Carly."

"Of course, sir." She gathers two menus along with a wine card. Zeke puts his hand at my lower back to nudge me to follow Carly as she exaggeratedly wiggles her curvy little ass—another eyeroll—all the way across the restaurant to the farthest table in the corner. I take in the layout, noting the restrooms are down a corridor which might lead to an exit. "Will this do, sir?" Carly asks.

"Perfectly."

He pulls my chair out and I sit. Carly doesn't spare me a glance as she leans deeply and holds the menus out to Zeke, her perky boobs almost popping out of her dress.

"We won't need those. We'll take two steaks, rare, and a bottle of—"

"Are you ordering for me?" I ask, interrupting.

He looks at me, eyebrows raised, and nods.

"Maybe I can have a look at the menu. Since it's 2024 and all." The last part I mutter as I pluck one of the menus out of Carly's hands and open it. Good thing they can't see my face over the top because the prices are insane. Everything is expensive. Even the chicken. Who pays that much for chicken? And I don't even know what some of the things are, so I close it and clear my throat.

"Yes. Steak for me too. Make mine well done, Carly," I say, holding the menu out to her. I smile wide as her lips curve downward in the corners. I'll eat dinner, then go to the bathroom while he pays the check. Slip out then.

She looks at the menu, then at Zeke, who nods. I didn't think I needed permission to order my dinner but okay.

"And a big plate of fries with extra ketchup." I turn to Zeke. "I'm not sharing. You'd better get your own."

He gives me a look but seems amused. "No fries for me. Bring her a vegetable too, will you? Steamed broccoli, I think."

I curl my lip although I don't mind broccoli. Carly takes the menus and Zeke orders a bottle of red.

"That's a lot of food," he says once Carly's gone.

"You're the one who ordered the broccoli."

"You need something green."

"Thanks for looking out for me. And, well, if you're paying, I may as well eat. Do you know how much a steak here costs?" I ask, looking around, taking in all the diners in their fancy clothes.

I tug the sleeves of my sweater down. I don't belong here.

"Does it intimidate you?"

"Hm? What?" I ask, turning to him.

"Does this place intimidate you?"

"No, I just think it's a waste. You can buy groceries for three weeks on the cost of one dinner and you don't have to deal with women like Carly. Although maybe you like women like Carly."

"Actually, I find them boring."

"Also that whole ordering for me? Seriously, do you get dates? Ever? Acting like that?"

"You'd be surprised." He takes a sip of water. "And you need red meat. Your iron's low."

"Pardon?"

"Bloodwork is back. It's probably why you have your dizzy spells."

That has me turning all my attention to him. "What?"

"Dizzy spells. Doctor thought it might be related."

"Is that what you were talking about when you left the room? My dizzy spells?"

He nods like it's normal but maybe for a man like him, a Society man, it is. A waiter arrives with rolls and butter, and another comes carrying a bottle of wine and two giant glasses. He pops the cork and pours for Zeke, talking some pretentious bullshit about the wine's origins as Zeke tastes it and gives his nod of approval. He pours for both of us and then leaves the bottle.

I pick up a roll and butter it. "It's not an iron deficiency."

"You are iron deficient."

"I can't normally afford steak." I pop bread into my mouth.

"I didn't realize you were medically trained."

"True, but that's not it."

"What is it then?"

I eat another bite of bread, not sure why I said anything. I pick up the glass of wine and sip and OMG it's good. Really good. I don't know much about wine, apart from cheap and this is not that.

"Don't chug it."

I give him a look and take another deliberately big sip, but I won't waste it. I set the glass down.

"You're classy, Blue."

"I don't want to cramp your style so I can leave if you prefer," I push my chair back and make to stand.

He sets his hand on my thigh, skin to skin contact

sending a bolt of electricity through me again. Does he feel it too? He has too, right? It can't just be me.

But I shouldn't forget even though he's the first man who's ever touched me or been interested in me in that way, he's probably had hundreds of women.

"Stay," he commands in that quiet, low way of his that leaves no room for anything but obedience.

I clear my throat and stay.

"The dizziness," he reminds me.

I shake my head to clear it and watch Carly lead another couple to their table. She glances at Zeke, and I look at him and I can see what she sees honestly. He's handsome, no doubt. Very handsome. Sexy in that rich asshole kind of way some women like. Hell, maybe I like it a little too, stupid as it is. He doesn't even glance her way, and I can admit she's a lot better looking than I am.

Zeke's gaze moves to my hand, and I realize I'm touching the scar on my face. I pull it away.

"My dad. The night he hurt Wren. I told you that he hit me, too. I didn't only break the mirror with my face." I point to the scar. "Bride of Frankenstein, remember? He smashed my head into the side of the tub. I don't know how many times. I passed out and ever since then, it just happens. It happens more when I'm stressed. And weirdly a lot when I'm around you," I tack on.

I have never told anyone this. Why am I telling him of all people? The bread I swallow sticks in my throat, and I gulp wine to wash it down.

"How did you take care of yourself and your sister? How did you afford it these last years?"

"How do you think? I worked. It's what normal people

do, Zeke. You're rich. You've never had to think about food or a roof over your head or a sick sister." His lips tighten and a shadow crosses his eyes. It takes him more than a minute before he blinks and the Zeke I am getting to know is back.

"What about school?"

I pick up another roll but just pick at it. I shake my head. I don't know why I feel embarrassed about this. I had zero options. It's not like I'm a drop out by choice.

"You never graduated high school?" he asks, sounding surprised.

"When would I have?" I snap, forcing myself to hold his gaze. Mom would tell me I have nothing to be ashamed of. I did what I had to do to take care of my family. But it's hard to keep my eyes on his. It's like he sees inside me, and I don't know how I feel about that. "Anyway, School of Hard Knocks, right?" I joke, look away. "Carly starting to look better to you?" I take off my sweater and drape it over the back of my chair, sweaty under his scrutinizing gaze not to mention anxious at what I have to do.

"You did it for your sister." It's not a question and I don't answer it. Instead, I lather butter on the roll.

"Aren't you hungry?" I ask him because he hasn't touched the bread.

"I don't usually eat this early."

"Then why are we?"

"I wanted to see something."

"What?"

Before he has a chance to answer, two waiters arrive at our table carrying our dinner, two gorgeous steaks, a huge plate of fries, salads, a side of bright green broccoli and more bread. It smells amazing and my stomach growls so loudly I'm sure everyone hears it.

As soon as the waiters are gone, I pick up my knife and fork and cut into my steak. Well, I attempt to, but the knife digs into the cut on my palm, and I put it down with a hiss of pain.

A small drop of blood appears along the cut. Zeke takes his napkin and puts it in my palm.

"Hold that," he says and, using his knife and fork, slices my steak while I watch, confused. Surprised. No, shocked. "There," he says when he's done. He pushes the plate back in front of me and I feel the warmth of tears in my eyes. I don't understand why. I look down at the steak cut into small bite-size pieces and remind myself my hand is cut because I made a shiv to protect myself against him. I can't feel tenderness or read into anything he does. He needs me to eat so I don't pass out. That's all this is. That is all.

I stab a piece of steak and put it into my mouth. The meat is tender, seasoned to perfection and grilled exactly like I like it and my appetite returns. I eat a second bite.

"There wasn't much food at your apartment," Zeke comments as he watches me before slicing into his steak.

"I ate at The Cat House. Best part of the job was the food."

"Was?"

"I'm pretty sure I'm fired. I was supposed to go in last night. Not that I planned on going back anyway."

"Why did you take a job there?"

"Money but also curiosity maybe. You were supposed

to be in Amsterdam. I didn't think I'd ever run into you. They paid great, so much better than any other job I could get, and..." I trail off and shrug my shoulders. I drink more of the wine and he refreshes my glass. "Once you paid, I was going to leave New Orleans. I like the place Wren's at now, so it made sense to work there. It's how I could afford her care. Anyhow, I don't know. This is good. Thanks."

He nods and we eat, conversation minimal. I've already said too much. And I realize I'm also drinking too much when he pours the last of the wine into my glass. I think he's barely had one refill.

His phone buzzes with a message as dessert comes, crème brûlée, a cappuccino for me and espresso for him. I break the glassy layer of burnt sugar and take a bite and wow. This is another level of delicious.

"Good?" he asks.

I guess I'd closed my eyes as the custard melted on my tongue. I nod. "You want to try it?"

He shakes his head. "No, I don't eat dessert."

"Why not?"

"I don't know."

"Maybe you should start. A little sweetness in your life might make you a happier person. Maybe—and I'm going to go out on a limb here, but maybe it'll even make you nice."

"Says the woman who tried to blackmail me." He shifts his gaze to his phone. "You're clean."

"Excuse me?"

"No STDs. Nothing wrong with your blood apart from the iron deficiency."

I'm glad my mouth isn't full or I'm sure I'd have spit out crème brûlée and that would be a waste.

"I could have told you that." I drink the last of my wine, wipe my mouth and sit back. "I tried to in fact."

"Finished?"

I nod.

He raises a hand and Carly, ever accommodating, comes rushing over. "Check please," he says, taking his wallet out of his jacket pocket.

"I'm going to run to the lady's room," I say, and slip away before he can stop me.

"Of course, sir," I hear her say as I hurry off, tote on my arm. I weave through the tables without looking back and make my way down the corridor bypassing the lady's room because I see the EXIT sign above the door at the end. It's a fire exit but someone has it propped open, and I can smell cigarette smoke. Probably the wait staff.

My ears ring with anxiety. I'm going so fast that when the men's room door opens, I almost collide with the man coming out, catching myself just in time as the waiter who delivered our dinner opens the exit door from outside and flips his cigarette onto the ground. A woman slips in under his arm, and I catch the door before it can close. I don't look back. Instead, as soon as I'm outside, I run. I run around the building, having to go farther than I hoped to get to where the taxis are lined up. The light turns red, but I bolt across the street, and someone honks their horn at me. I don't care, though. I reach a taxi and the driver disconnects his call as I open the back door.

"Go! Please go!" I set one leg inside, the strap of the tote catching on the door handle.

"Where to?"

"Just go!" I tug at the bag, get it loose. I'm about to shut the door when a hand closes over the top of it, stopping me, and Ezekiel St. James leans down, eyes narrowed, jaw set. He takes hold of my arm.

"Going somewhere, Little Convict?"

21

EZEKIEL

I toss a hundred-dollar bill into the front seat of the taxi and drag Blue out.

"Let me go!" she cries out.

I keep hold of her arm and march her back to the SUV, unlocking it as we approach.

"I'll scream. I swear I'll scream."

I open the passenger door and spin her to face me. "You do that. You try. And I'll swap you out for your sister."

Emotions ravage her face, fear and rage and frustration as she opens her mouth, closes it again.

"Get your ass in the fucking car," I hiss, depositing her inside before she has a chance to obey. Or not. Most likely not. I strap her in then take the chain she has hidden beneath her dress out and bind her to the bar on the dash. I slam her door shut and stalk across the front to my side and get in.

I am fuming. I am so fucking angry. Angry at her. At myself. What the fuck was I thinking in there? We were on some fucking date? Why in fuck's name did I let her slip away to the bathroom?

"This isn't safe!" she cries out as I pull out of the spot, cars behind us honking their horns when I cut them off.

I glance at her. Her head is bent forward, and she's got the chain in one hand to give herself some slack but it's short and she can't sit up.

"No, I guess it isn't." I speed out of the city as Blue hangs on for dear life.

"Slow down! Jesus. Slow down!"

I don't. I keep my eyes on the road and drive double the speed limit until we reach the house. Blue is gripping the bar on the dash, and I make sure to block her view of the keypad as I punch in the numbers to open the gate then drive up to the pitch-black house. I park and look at her, still fuming, still so fucking furious. Only thing is I'm not sure which of us I'm angrier with.

I climb out, slam the door shut muttering a curse as I force myself to take a deep breath in then out before stalking to her side and opening her door. I unlock the chain and instead of letting her walk, I reach in to take hold of her and lift her out, then haul her over my shoulder.

"What the fuck! Let me fucking go, you asshole!" She pounds on my back, and I smack her ass hard, making her yelp. I stomp up the stairs to the imposing, ugly front entrance of Carlton Bishop's house, punch in the code to unlock the door and enter. I don't bother to put on any lights but make my way upstairs in the dark.

"What are you doing? What the hell are you doing,

Zeke?" she calls out, panic in her voice as she bounces on my shoulder.

I set her down outside her bedroom door. She stumbles backward into the wall. I lean into her. Her eyes are saucers staring up at me, the cocky, funny girl from dinner gone, this terrified version of Blue in her place.

"You mistake me for a fool." I grip her dress and tug hard once, tearing it in two. She screams when I spin her around rip it from her, stripping her, doing the same with her bra and panties. I turn her to face me again.

She presses her back to the wall, hands flat against it.

"Zeke—"

"What did I tell you about that?" I ask, lifting her, tossing her over my shoulder once more as I carry her into the bedroom, kicking the door closed behind me and tossing her onto the bed.

She bounces once, scrambles to her hands and knees to get away.

I capture her ankle and yank her back. She falls flat on her stomach. I tug her to the edge of the bed, so her legs hang off the end, set one knee on her lower back and smack her ass hard three times. She cries out. I strip off my jacket, roll my sleeve up to my elbows, undo the top buttons of my shirt.

"Please. Please." She's half-turned on the bed, pinned by my knee.

I begin spanking her ass. She struggles beneath me, but her strength is no match for mine. And I'm pretty sure the punishment she's taking tonight makes last night's look like a fucking game. Her ass burns bright red and my hand stings.

"What the fuck were you thinking? Playing me for a fucking fool!"

"You're not! I wasn't. I swear!" She manages to crawl partially up the bed. I drag her back, lift her. She weighs nothing. I carry her to the wall, trap her between it and my body. She wraps her legs around my middle as I grip her hair and force her head backward.

"Flirting like you were."

"I wasn't!"

"Telling me what you told me about your father. What he did. Was it all so I let my guard down?"

She shakes her head, pulls at my hair, exhausted and panting. Both of us panting. I look at her face, her tear-stained cheeks.

"It wasn't," she says. "I swear. I've never told anyone what I've told you."

I stare at her, hearing her ragged breaths, confused, angry, furious. Wanting. And in the next moment, I'm kissing her. My mouth is on hers and I'm fucking kissing her and she's kissing me back, and I can't get enough. I can't fucking get enough.

I fist a handful of hair and tug her head backward to look at her. She's panting, lips swollen. She stares up at me with those too-blue, too-sad eyes, eyes that I think I can lose myself in, and then I'm on her again, locked in a frenzied kiss, Blue all lips and tongue and then, and then, cutting teeth.

I draw back, touch my hand to my lip. It comes away bloody and she does not look sorry.

"You want to fight, Little Convict?"

I carry her to the bed, lay her down. I lay my weight

on top of her and look down at her face, her hair in tangles, that scar visible after the mess of our war.

Her breath comes in pants. She's worn out but looks at me through narrowed eyes, not giving up just yet. I reach over my head and strip off my shirt. She stares up at me, her gaze moving over my chest, my arms, the part of the twin dragons visible to her. Lower to my abs, the trail of hair that disappears into my slacks.

"You're mine, Blue," I say, undoing my belt, the button of my pants. "You belong to me."

She watches as I step off the bed, unzip my slacks and push them along with my briefs down and off.

Her gaze moves to my cock, then up to my face, then back. She licks her lips, her eyes huge and dark, the blue a ring around black pupils.

"It's time I showed you what that means."

22

BLUE

He stands naked, letting me look, letting me take in the whole of him. I'm up on my elbows and all I can do is stare because I've never seen anyone that looks like him. He is so beautiful. So brutally beautiful.

Broad shoulders give way to sculpted arms around which the scaly ink of twin dragons circle, meeting, I guess, at his back because I can see their bodies curled up along his shoulders. His chiseled abs look cut from stone, perfectly defined as they flex with every move. I can't keep my eyes from following that dark trail of hair just below his belly button down to his cock and fuck me.

It's huge.

"Ezekiel," I say, making a point of using his whole name because I do not need to piss him off any more than I already have. It's like those dragons inked onto his flesh, the twin beasts, have woken. And they're due a reckoning.

"Better," he says, fisting his cock, rubbing the length

of it as I stare. I lick my lips because there's something wrong with me. Because that flutter in my belly? It's nerves and arousal. Not fear. Not wholly fear, at least. How can I feel what I'm feeling when I look at him? He's my kidnapper. My captor.

He grips my legs, tugs me to the edge of the bed, making me fall flat on my back. His fingers dig into my thighs, which he keeps spread wide as he steps between them.

"Do you remember which hole I told you I'd take first?"

Panic animates me and I try to kick free of his grasp, and he almost laughs, it's so easy for him to overpower me. He's twice my size and so strong. So much stronger than me.

"Please! You can't! I've never…"

"I know you've never," he says, his gaze dropping between my legs. "It makes this so much more interesting." With one quick, practiced move, he flips me onto my stomach. My feet touch the carpet as he takes both wrists in one of his hands. I crane my neck to look back at him. He nudges my knees wider with his and smacks my ass again.

I yelp. It fucking stings.

But then his fingers move over my pussy, and I freeze when they brush against my clit.

"I think, Blue," he starts, glancing at me before shifting his gaze back to my ass. "I think I change my mind. A reprieve for you. For tonight."

I'm not sure what he means. Is he not going to fuck me? A glance at his very hard cock tells me that's not it.

"I think," he says, fingers moving, making me rise on tiptoe and press my belly into the bed. "Tonight, I'd like to soak my dick in virgin blood." He shifts his gaze to mine and holds it.

"I have my period," I say, stupidly, naïvely thinking that will get me out of what's coming, not even sure I want to get out of it.

"Oh, well then," he starts and I almost exhale with relief or disappointment but then he chuckles and glances down once more. I gasp when I feel rather than see what he does next. When he tugs on the string and pulls my tampon out. "What's a little more blood?"

He drops the tampon on the floor, and, as if to prove his point, he swipes two fingers over my opening and brings them, smeared with blood, to his mouth and licks.

"Oh my God."

He grins. "I'm not afraid of a little blood, sweetheart. I may even like it."

"Zeke?" I start and it's the wrong thing to say.

He spins me onto my back, grips my thighs and pushes my legs so wide, I think they're going to snap. He leans close toward me, so close I can see the specks of silver and midnight in the gray of his eyes. "What did I say about that?"

"I'm sorry. Ezekiel. I mean Ezekiel."

"Better."

"I don't think," I start but stop when he bends his head and what he does next so surprises me that the words catch in my throat because he swipes his tongue over my clit before taking it between his teeth.

I suck in a shaky breath, fisting the sheets as I squeeze

my eyes shut because I've never felt anything like this before. No one has ever done this to me. The softness of his tongue, the rough stubble along his cheek, it all feels I don't know, I don't fucking know, and when he closes his lips over that swollen nub and sucks, I moan and arch my back, pressing myself into his face because I want more.

No. I *need* more.

"Oh... God!"

He lifts his head. "Don't come just yet, sweetheart," he says, sucking hard once more before straightening, his lips glistening, wet with me. He grins, steps close enough to nestle his cock between my legs and all I can do is watch him and try to take some control of all these feelings, the sensations as he rubs his length between my folds. He takes my hands and puts them on his shoulders then bends my knees back while I stare up at him, the heat of his body against mine, the firm muscle of his shoulders, his biceps. He reaches one arm beneath me and adjusts my position to better accommodate himself, I guess, and pushes my legs even wider before shifting his gaze down between us.

His cock presses warm and hard at my entrance.

"This is going to hurt," he says, and before I can even register the meaning of his words, before I can prepare myself, he thrusts inside me.

All the way inside me.

When I feel the barrier give, I cry out with the sudden, sharp pain. He moans, the sound something animal coming from deep inside his chest, as warmth coats my insides.

Blood. My virgin blood.

"Zeke. Oh God. Zeke. Please. It hurts." His name is a breath on my lips. My fingernails dig into his shoulders, drawing his blood, bleeding him like he is me.

His breath is ragged and he's holding still. I look at his face and I see how much effort it's taking for him to be still. He meets my eyes, bites his lower lip, and with what I can only describe as a growl, he draws back only to thrust again. I cry out as he draws me up and closes his mouth over mine. He moans, and kisses me hard and does it again, forcing the air from my lungs.

"Fuck. Blue. Fuck." He shudders, brings the thumb of one hand to my clit and the instant he does, everything changes. Every fucking sensation like a tidal wave taking me under. He moves inside me, deep and hard, and his thumb, it circles my clit, rubs it. Pleasure is edged with pain, warm and wet between my legs, the moaning mine, not his. And I realize I'm going to come.

He's going to make me come.

But then he pulls out with a grin.

I protest. He knew. He fucking knew.

"Not yet. You don't deserve it just yet, do you?" He flips me over, gets on his knees on the bed and hauls my hips high. With one hand he grips my hair and pushes my face down into the bed before he starts fucking me from behind, fingers of one hand on my clit again, the other digging into the flesh of my ass as he splays me wide and when I turn to watch him, he's watching himself fuck me and he's so beautiful. He's so fucking beautiful like this. Sweat glistens on his forehead, his lips are swollen and his eyes, his eyes have gone black. When they meet mine, there's a darkness to them, a desire so insatiable, so wild, it makes my insides quake.

"You're mine, Blue," he groans. "Mine. All mine," he says, fucking turning frenzied, hard and fast and deep and I am out of control.

"I'm going to come," I cry out, the sensations over-whelming, like nothing I've ever experienced before and as I watch him, his beautiful face, sweat dripping from his forehead onto my back, this man, my captor, my enemy, I come. I come so hard the world goes black around the edges as orgasm passes in waves through me, making me his, making me only his. Making me *want to be his*.

He bends over me, body warm and solid at my back and closes his mouth over the curve of my neck. He stills. I hear a muttered curse against my skin. His breath is hot and warm, his tongue wet. Fingers dig into tender flesh. His cock throbs and I feel the spurting of come inside me and there is nothing else I want right now but to take it. My pussy pulses around his cock, milking it, greedy for more and when he's empty, he collapses on top of me, panting. He stays like that for a long, long moment, then rolls onto his side, one arm around my middle so my back is to his front, and he's still inside me. He holds me like this, and I grip the arm that presses me to him, panting and shivering, sweat cooling on our bodies as I try to understand what the fuck just happened between us.

23

EZEKIEL

When I pull away from Blue, she makes a sound and leans against me, holding onto the arm I have draped across her stomach, which surprises me. I still and only when her grip loosens do I draw out from inside her. A rush of blood and come spills onto her thighs and mine, stains the once pristine sheets a dark red.

Blue is shivering. I stand, look down at her. I pick up the chain attached to her collar and bind her to the bed then pull the blanket up over her. I don't say a word. Not yet. I don't know what to say.

What the fuck was that? I meant to take her, to bend her over and take her and show her who she belonged to. I did not intend on allowing her to come. And I certainly did not intend on kissing her. Holding her.

I walk into the bathroom and shut the door behind me.

What the fuck was that?

I grip the edge of the counter and look at myself in

the mirror. My face is scratched, my lips are swollen and cut. My shoulders and biceps, too, are decorated with crescent-moon marks left by her fingernails. That I expected. I took her hard. I felt her resistance, and pushed through the barrier and claimed her as mine.

Mine.

What the fuck?

I rake a hand through my hair before turning away from my reflection and switching on the shower. I should have done as I promised and taken her ass. She wouldn't hold on to me then, I am sure. I couldn't though. The look in her eyes, the scent of her, the promise of virgin blood, it was too much. Too irresistible.

And I didn't want to hurt her. As tight as she is, I'd have split her in two if I'd taken her ass. She'll need to be prepared to take me there because as much as I hate to admit it, I wanted to watch her come undone. I wanted her to cling to me. To want me.

To want me.

Fuck.

I don't fucking understand.

The road to hell is paved with good intentions. That's the expression, right? I just need to remember that to allow her pleasure, to make her come, doesn't make me any less of what I am.

The beast pillaging the virgin half his size.

I swipe my finger over her blood drying on my dick, my thighs and bring it to my mouth. I lick it off. Sick. I know. But there should be no doubt that I am that beast.

Water runs pink down the drain washing away her

blood. The dark thing inside me likes the look of it, one word repeating over and over in my head.

Mine.

I've had a lot of women, but not one of them was a virgin. Well, apart from my first. We were kids then, both of us sixteen. I didn't know what I was doing. Tonight, what I did, I did fully aware.

It doesn't mean anything, I tell myself, turning my face up to the flow of water. It's just bodies. Just fucking. Virgin or not, pussy is pussy. That's all. That's all it's been for me for a very long time.

But kissing her. Fuck. Kissing her. I couldn't stop, even when she bit me. I couldn't stop kissing her and to think of it now makes me want it again.

I switch off the shower and grab a towel, wiping water from my face and hair. The mirror has fogged so I don't have to look at myself. Wrapping the towel low over my hips, I return to the bedroom to find Blue sitting up in the bed. She's hugging her knees and although the blanket is pulled tight around her, she's shivering. Her hair is wild, her lips are swollen, her eyes a little lost. A lot accusing.

Guilt gnaws at me, twists something inside me. I'm about to ask her if she's all right, but my cell phone rings from inside my jacket pocket, and I cross the room to pick it up. When I see it's Jericho, I answer.

"Yeah," I say. I feel her eyes on me as I walk out of the room.

"Where are you?"

"At the house."

"The girl?"

"Here too. Where would she be?"

"We're coming over."

"Why?"

"She needs to answer some questions."

"What questions?"

"I'll tell you when we get there."

"I need half an hour."

"Why?"

"Because."

"Fine."

This seems to be how conversations with my brother go these days.

I disconnect and walk down the hall into the bedroom where Cynthia unpacked some of my things that Jericho had sent over. I pull on a pair of jeans, a light V-neck sweater, socks and shoes. I comb my hair and bring my hands to my nose. Her scent lingers there. It's faint, but it's there. At least I think I'm not imagining it.

Jesus. What the fuck is wrong with me?

There's a bathtub in this room. I'll wash her. Make sure she's all right. The bathroom in Blue's room only has the shower stall. I run a bath, testing the temperature, and plugging the tub. As it fills up, I walk back out into the hallway and see Blue's ruined clothes on the floor, that tote bag on its side. I pick up the tote, her under-things, the ruined dress. When I do, though, something falls out of her pocket. I stop, look at it. It's a rolled-up wad of cash that's been rubber-banded together.

What the fuck? I bend to pick it up, take off the rubber band. At a quick glance, there's another grand, maybe two here.

That guilt of moments ago evaporates. I stalk into the

bedroom where Blue hasn't moved. Granted, she can't. But that's what you get when you try to run.

"What the fuck is this?" I ask, holding up the money.

She looks at it, her mouth falling open.

"Where did you get this, Blue?"

"I'm really cold. And I need to use the bathroom," she says, trying to sound defiant but I see how her lower lip is trembling, how her eyes are filling up, the skin around them already pink. She is at my mercy. She is more mine than she can possibly understand. That twisting in my gut is back at the sight of her like this.

Helpless.

Defenseless.

The man I've become over the years is a cold, wretched thing, a beast. Maybe it's the last shred of anything human inside me, anything that feels, but seeing her like this softens me. With a sigh, I reach to unhook the chain from her collar. When I do, I expect her to scurry away, but she doesn't. She remains as she is looking at me. Is she waiting for permission?

"I'm running a bath for you in the other room. Come." I hold out my hand.

She doesn't move.

"Come Blue. It will be more comfortable for you."

"Why?"

"Why what?"

"Why would you care if something is more comfortable for me?"

"Honestly?" I push my hand through my hair. "I have no fucking idea, but I do."

She studies me and I find I can't look at her. Instead, I

gather up the throw draped over the arm of a chair and hold it out for her. She gets up, and I see the blood that's dried on her thighs. She steps into the blanket, and I wrap it around her shoulders. She shivers as I lead her out to the room next door and when we reach the bathroom, the tub is half full. I sit on the edge to test the water again before standing and offering her a hand.

She ignores it and gets in on her own, discarding the blanket, her back to me. Her ass still bears the imprint of my hand. I don't miss her hiss when she sits and watch the water turn pink as she rubs blood off her thighs.

Seeing this, her like this? Well, I am exactly the asshole she accuses me of being.

"I should have been gentler. I hurt you. I didn't want to hurt you."

"Yeah, you did. You wanted to punish me, to show me that you are in control, and you did. At least be honest about it."

"That's not..." I trail off, dropping it. I remind myself she's keeping secrets from me. Playing me for a fool. "Where's the money from?"

"The apartment. I kept it separate of the rest in case anyone ever broke in. Never put all your eggs in one basket." From behind I see her wipe her face. She's crying. Again.

"At the restaurant why did you run?" Because I don't like how I felt about her running. Because in some way, maybe I thought, well, fuck. Who the fuck knows what I thought? My brain is fucking broken and I'm not making any fucking sense, not when it comes to Blue.

She glances over her shoulder at me, shakes her head

then turns back, picking up the bottle of body wash and squeezing some onto her hands to wash herself. She looks, in a word, defeated.

This is not what I want.

I cross the room to sit on the edge of the tub and take the body wash. She only resists momentarily but gives it up. I pour some onto my hands and begin to wash her, taking care with her, feeling her soft, vulnerable flesh beneath my hands.

She remains silent as I finish washing her. She looks up at me when I hold out my hand, palm up, and takes it, letting me help her out of the tub. Water cascades over her skin before I wrap her in a towel and turn her to face me, holding onto her.

"Tell me why you ran."

"Do you just expect me not to try? To just be your puppet, do what you say?"

"We have an arrangement."

"*You* have an arrangement. *I* have no choice."

"I told you—"

"Do you think that I don't know what you can do to me?" she snaps. "Do you think I'm not fully aware you could twist my neck and the effort wouldn't even make you break a sweat? You could then dump my body somewhere on the grounds here, hell, you don't even have to bury me it's so vast. And who would come looking for me? No one. No one would know. No one would care. Well, one person would. But she can't come looking, can she? And tell me something else. Say that happens..." Emotion makes her falter.

"It's not going to."

"Say it does. What happens to her? What happens to my sister who has already lost so much?" she asks, tears streaming down her face that she wipes at angrily. "What happens to Wren when the checks that pay for her care stop coming? What do you think they do with her? Keep her there out of the goodness of their hearts? That's not how this world works, *Zeke*."

"It's not going to get to that point."

"Have you ever seen a state-run facility? Do you know the shit that happens there? Especially to those who have no one to stand up for them. No one to look after them and care about them."

"You're getting yourself worked up."

"No, I'm not. I'm just being realistic." She breaks free of my hold. "So, if you're pissed I tried to run, too bad for you." She sets her jaw stubbornly. "I would do it again if I had the chance!"

"There she is, my Little Convict."

"I'm not yours." She tries to shove past me.

I capture her arm. "Oh, but you are. You're mine and if you try something like that again—"

"What? What will you do, Zeke? Spank me?"

I narrow my eyes, study her features, those cerulean eyes that have seen so much evil and yet manage to remain so innocent in their own way. So fucking naïve.

But naïve can get a girl killed. Doesn't she know that?

"You need me, Blue. More than you realize."

"Let me go."

"And no, I wouldn't spank you to punish you. You like that too much."

"Fuck you."

"That, too, you like too much," I say, attempting to smile. I expect her to deny it. I prepare myself for her to, but she only flushes pink, glances away. "And I like it too much." I walk her backward to the wall and cage her in. "I like it too much, Blue." I kiss her mouth and the twisting in my gut of earlier morphs into something else. Something with wings. I draw back to look at her searching, wounded eyes. "We have an arrangement, you and me. I don't break my word. I will protect you. I will keep you safe from your father and anyone else who tries to hurt you. I swear it. Do you understand?"

"Zeke—"

"In exchange you will give me back my duffel bag and once I'm certain you don't have more on that little computer of yours that can endanger my family or myself, we'll see about next steps."

"No. Not we'll see about next steps. Next steps means you let me go once you realize there's nothing more."

"Let you go how? Penniless? What will you do? Get Wren and what? I saw your car in the parking lot of the apartment. At least I'm pretty sure it's yours given the license plates. Does it even run?"

"It's fine."

"You have no money. No mode of transport."

"I have some money."

"Two grand won't cut it. Not if you want to give Wren the kind of help she needs."

"What are you proposing then?"

"You stay with me. Do as you're told. We handle this. Figure it all out. You need my help not only for yourself but for Wren. I'll make sure Wren is properly cared for."

She opens her mouth, closes it again. Her expression is confused. "Why would you do that?" she finally asks. "Why would you help me?"

I study her face, search her eyes. How do I answer this? "Because I wasn't able to help someone else, before you." I feel my throat close up. I clench my teeth and swallow the pain of my chest tightening. Am I telling her this? Am I saying it? "And she died," I hear the words come out of my mouth and I feel as stunned as she looks.

Blue's eyes fill like wells.

"But you have to trust me, Blue. You can't do what you did tonight. You're not safe. You don't know everything."

"What does that mean?"

"You have to trust me. And if not me, well, then trust my motives are selfish if that makes it easier to swallow. I am alleviating my own guilt by helping you. Think of it as my atonement."

"I don't understand."

"You don't have to. You only have to accept and agree."

"What did that mean? That I don't know everything?"

"Your father made parole. He'll be out of prison within two weeks."

24

BLUE

"What?" It's like someone sideswiped me. My mouth falls open, that ringing beginning in my ears. I close my eyes, breathe. I need to keep control of myself. I can't have one of my spells, not now.

"He made parole."

"How? That's not possible. He barely served any time. He—"

"Shh." Zeke takes my arms. "He can't leave the state of Pennsylvania. At least not without permission or he violates his parole. You should be safe here."

"But I'm not. Wren's not." I look up at him. "Are you lying? So I agree? Because I'll agree anyway. I don't have many options. Hell, I don't have any options."

He shakes his head. "I'm not lying, Blue. Get dressed. My brother and Robbie are on their way over. They have some questions apparently."

"What questions?"

"Not sure."

"Zeke? You upstairs?" Comes a man's deep voice from somewhere in the house, startling me.

"Be down in a sec," Zeke calls out, gray eyes on me. "Take a few minutes. Get dressed and come downstairs."

"This is all so bad." I press the heels of my hands into my eyes. He's getting out. He warned me he has powerful contacts. They must have helped him get out.

"No one is going to come near you or Wren, Blue. Get dressed. Come downstairs."

"Can I have my phone back?" I ask him.

"Why?"

"Don't worry, I won't call an Uber or something. Just want to call Rudy, make sure Wren's okay. Make sure he knows no one gets in to see her." His eyes narrow. He doesn't trust me. I get it. I wouldn't trust me either. But can I count on him to get me out of this, to keep us safe? "You want me to start trusting you. You need to start trusting me too. I'm only asking for my phone so I can communicate with my sister."

"I'll think about it. Get dressed."

With a sigh, I nod, and he leaves, closing the door behind himself. I take a minute to process.

My dad is getting out of prison. Zeke's right that he isn't allowed to cross state lines but that's not going to stop him. Not if it means life or death because the man who wants those files will kill him. I know that.

At that, I rush out of the bathroom and back to my bedroom. On the nightstand is the wad of cash. It's not that I'm concerned about right now, though. The ruined dress is on the bed. I close the door behind me and pick it up to check the pockets and I have never been as relieved as I am in this moment. Because there, stuck on a loose string in the pocket, is the flash drive.

It didn't fall out. Zeke doesn't know about it.

This is my back up plan. It has to be. I trust Zeke's intentions. I believe he will help me and if it's only to alleviate his own guilt, so be it. I saw how dark his eyes went when he told me that. In helping me, he hopes to atone for a past sin. A failure that cost someone their life. I have a feeling it has to do with Zoë, whoever she is. I remember how he got when I asked about her. Remember what his brother said to him. Maybe I remind him of her. Was she a girlfriend or something?

I shake my head. That doesn't matter. None of that matters. Him helping me doesn't mean he cares about me, and the fucking? Well, that's just a bonus for him.

It's not that I want him to care or anything like that. Although there's something with him. I don't know. Maybe it's just how big he is. How powerful. How much in control. Hell, maybe it's just that we've been intimate. He's my first and my emotions are mixed up. My broken brain trying to make something out of nothing. Like when he cut the steak for me at the restaurant or how he checks that my hand is healing well.

It's all confusing.

No. I shake my head. I chalk it up to emotions being high. I can't be stupid, even though I will admit that on some level, it's a relief to have his protection. I need to remember why I'm here. He has no loyalty to me, the opposite if anything. I tried to blackmail him. He doesn't know me. I'm nothing to him.

As good as his intentions may be, he doesn't know the

kind of people dad was dealing with. The kind that will put a gun to a sixteen-year-old girl's head. The kind that will pull the trigger if they got the chance. I know that. I was there for it. Played the leading role.

I don't know what is on this flash drive. I haven't been able to access more than a few files. I don't even want to know more. But if the only way Wren and I will be safe will be to give it back to whoever wants it, then I'll do that.

I get dressed quickly, pulling on my worn but beloved jeans and a sweater. I should have taken some shoes from my apartment, too, but I just slip my feet into these borrowed ballet flats. I bury the flash drive inside the pocket of my jeans and make sure it's not visible before I head out into the hallway and down the stairs. I can already hear men's voices coming from the study, where light spills out of the open door. My heart beats fast as I make my way to it.

There's nothing they could have found on that laptop. There's nothing to find. I don't know what questions they'll have for me, but I should be safe. And once they're gone, I'll ask Zeke for one more thing. To move Wren and maybe Rudy, too. To bring them here? No, that's too hard. I need her somewhere where I can get us out if I need to. This house is a fortress.

Taking a deep breath in, I enter the study. Three sets of eyes turn to me, conversation coming to an abrupt halt the moment I'm inside.

Zeke is leaning against the desk drinking a whiskey. His brother, Jericho, whom I recognize from the other day, is standing with his arm on the mantle of the fireplace. He, too, is holding a tumbler of whiskey. A man I don't know is sitting on the couch with my laptop on his lap, that gun in its Ziploc on the coffee table beside a bottle of whiskey and an empty tumbler. A fire is burning in the fireplace. It's not a cold night but it's comforting hearing the crackling of wood.

I clear my throat.

"Come inside, Blue," Zeke tells me.

I go to stand next to him. He puts his drink down and wraps a hand around the back of neck to lead me toward the others.

"Sit down," Zeke says. "Jericho, Robbie, this is Blue. Blue, my brother, Jericho and Robbie."

I nod, wipe my sweaty hands on my jeans.

"Relax," he whispers. He walks over to the desk and picks up his whiskey, makes a point of taking a sip while I watch, then hands it to me. He's making sure I know it's not drugged. I take it, although I don't like the stuff, especially after the other night, and drink a sip. He's right, I need to relax. They don't know anything. Hell, I hardly know anything.

"Where did you get the laptop?" Jericho asks.

"I already told you, it was her father's," Zeke says.

His brother's eyes, which are different colors, are zeroed in on me like he's trying to read my mind. "I'd like to hear it from her," he says with a quick glance in his brother's direction.

I wonder about the dynamic between them. I think Jericho is older but they're close in age. What is their relationship like? The two times I've seen them together it seems tense. There's some unresolved history between them.

"It's my father's," I repeat.

"And the gun?"

"My father's." I scratch my nose and look up at Zeke who narrows his eyes.

"Well, that's odd," Jericho says.

Zeke folds his arms, leaning against the mantle alongside his brother.

"How so?" I ask.

"How so, Robbie?" Jericho mimics.

"Thanks for asking," Robbie says. Is this some game to them? Robbie continues typing something onto the laptop, so it takes him a moment to drag his gaze to mine. "Funny enough, it's registered to Imperium Valens Invictum. New Orleans chapter."

I'm confused. *Imperium Valens Invictum.* "Am I supposed to know what that is?" I ask, shifting my gaze from the man to Zeke.

"IVI. The Society," he says.

The Society, as in his secret society. As in The Cat House and whatever else they have going on behind those high walls.

"That doesn't make any sense. How do you even know? The serial number is filed off."

"Not well enough," Robbie says.

"So, unless your father is a member of The Society, and I'm pretty sure he's not, you're lying," Jericho says, accusation loud and clear. He does not like me.

My throat goes dry, my stomach twisting in knots as I look up at Zeke whose face is stone.

"Explain yourself," Jericho says.

"Where did you get the gun, Blue?" Zeke asks.

"I—"

Zeke crosses the room so fast, I gasp and lean as far back in the chair as I can. He grips a handful of hair and tugs my head backward. I wrap both hands around his forearm.

"We made a deal, you and me. Not five fucking minutes ago. I'm done with your lies. You tell the truth, now, or it's off."

"What does that mean?"

"It means you lose my protection. Your sister loses my protection."

"You can't do that."

"No? What did I tell you upstairs about playing me for a fool?"

"I'm not. I swear. Let go. You're hurting me."

He looks at me. I'm half off my seat trying to alleviate the pressure on my scalp. He releases me but doesn't move away.

I rub my scalp and see how Jericho is watching us. I get the feeling he wants to know what's going on between his brother and me. I get the feeling he won't like it that we fucked.

"I never told you it was my dad's," I say to Zeke. "You assumed and when you asked me I just—"

"You just lied. Which you seem to do fairly casually."

I shake my head, look down at my lap, try to think. I wipe my eyes because this is going from bad to worse and I have a feeling we're just getting started.

"Whose gun is it?" Jericho asks.

Jericho looks angry and like he's not surprised. Zeke, though, there's more there. Not just anger.

"I don't know," I say, my voice sounding more fragile than usual. At least the answer is true. "Can I?" I point to the whiskey and Zeke nods, so I pick it up and drink a sip. I hold onto it, to have something to do with my hands.

"Continue," Zeke says.

I look up at them and I know I am in so far over my head. This world, I don't belong here. These men are dangerous. So dangerous.

"Blue, last fucking chance."

I nod. "After my dad was arrested, I left. I took my mom's car and Wren and I left. I was in a hurry and scared and hadn't thought it through. I had no money. I was sixteen. And Wren, well, my big sister was gone. She was always good at taking care of us and the Wren I knew was gone." My hands shake as I bring the tumbler to my lips and force myself to swallow past the lump in my throat. "I knew where Mom hid her checkbook and there wasn't a lot of money but some, so I went back to the house to get it. It was late and no one should have been there, but someone was." My voice breaks as I recall that night. What almost happened. "Two men."

"Who were they?" Zeke asks.

I shrug my shoulders. "They didn't take the time to introduce themselves," I say, trying for casual but failing. "The house was torn apart. I was stunned. When I walked in, I mean, I just stood there, and he was right there although he didn't see me at first. If I'd been faster, I maybe could have run. But then another man came out of the bedroom. He saw me right away. And he said something, I don't know what. I tried to run then but I was too slow. The first man, he grabbed me, and held me while the other one asked me where it was."

"Where what was?" Jericho asks.

I point to the laptop. "He said my dad had left something for him, but it wasn't where it was supposed to be. I knew that much. I'd already taken it. I couldn't tell him where it was or they'd find Wren. When I wouldn't give him the answer he wanted, he just got bored or something. He checked his watch like he was late. Then he told the other one to take care of me and left. And then he, the one who was left behind..." Oh God. This part. This next part. Another secret I've kept, like what happened to Wren. What my father did to her before he beat her.

"Blue?" Zeke says gentler this time. "What did he do?"

I don't look up. I keep my eyes on the amber liquid in the glass. "He grinned and it was the scariest thing I'd ever seen. He took me into the bedroom and threw me on the bed and... He hit me. Slapped me and I was dazed. He didn't have to. He was so much bigger than me and so strong." I drag in a shaky breath and in my periphery, I see how Zeke's hands are clenched, his body stiff. "I guess he decided since he couldn't find the laptop that he'd take something else while he was there. He'd had his gun out already to threaten me with it and he set it aside. He then... When he had his hand in..." Jesus. I look away from them. All of them. I take a shaky breath, start again. "He told me what he was going to do to me, and I could see he would. He was..." My voice is so small, so shaky. I've never talked about this. "He undid my jeans and when he put his hand inside, I didn't even think. I just grabbed the gun. It was right there, and I grabbed it, and I don't even know how it went off. I don't know."

"Christ." Zeke pushes his hands into his pockets.

"Did you kill him?" Jericho asks.

"I didn't know at first. I thought maybe. He was so heavy on me, and it took forever to get him off but then he made a sound, and I think I'd only hit his shoulder or something. I don't know. There was a lot of blood, but I didn't wait for him to wake up. I just grabbed the checkbook I'd come for, and I ran. I didn't even realize I was still holding onto the gun until I got to the motel."

I rub my face, press the heels of my hands into my eyes. I still remember how it felt to have him on top of me. I can still feel his hand inside my panties.

"What did he look like?" Jericho asks, some of the edge gone from his voice.

I shake my head. I don't want to remember. "Blond hair. Really light, like his eyes. Big too. He had a tattoo on his neck. Here." I point behind my ear, to the side of my neck. "An O with something like a plus sign through it."

Zeke and Jericho exchange a glance.

"Draw it," Jericho says, getting up to retrieve a piece of paper and pencil from the desk.

"Um. Okay. It was something like this, I think. I remember because it was kind of familiar but I'm not sure why."

I draw the symbol. Jericho looks at it, clearly doesn't know what it is. The man with the laptop speaks up.

"It's called a coda."

"What is that?" Jericho asks.

"Like from a sheet of music?" I ask, realizing why I found it familiar. "I took music classes at school. It was mandatory. That's probably why I recognized it. I don't remember what it stood for though."

"Finale," the man fills in, still busy on the laptop.

"Didn't know you studied music," Zeke says to him.

"I am a man of many interests," he says with a smile.

"And the other man?" Zeke asks.

I shake my head. "I couldn't see his face. Just heard his voice. He had a long coat on and a hat. There was something though. I'm not sure, it was dark, but I think he only had one hand."

"How do you know that?"

"His coat, it was pinned where his right hand should have been."

Another glance is exchanged between the brothers.

"I know my father was in over his head. What he'd done this time, stealing what he stole, it was not his usual kind of job. He was small time, and this one was going to be his jackpot, he'd said. But I know he was afraid of whoever he was working for, too."

Robbie turns the laptop around. "There were a lot of files on this computer once. Looks like they were moved to an external drive."

My heart leaps. How the fuck does he know that?

"Some that were in a buried file I've been able to retrieve but I'm guessing there are more. Any idea where that external drive might be?"

Yeah. In my pocket. I don't say that though. I sit on my hands, trying to stop them from shaking and shake my head. "I guess my dad had moved them." I lean my nose into my shoulder to scratch it. When I look up, I see Zeke's eyes intently watching me. They narrow a little.

"I think Blue is tired," he says suddenly, stepping away from the mantle.

I get up to my feet, nod, grateful to get out of here.

Jericho watches us, quiet but observing, not missing a thing.

Zeke walks over to the desk and retrieves something from inside the drawer. He comes to me, and I see it's my phone.

"Code is 84651. Check on your sister then go to bed, understand? Do not make me regret giving this to you."

I take the phone, look up at him, grateful again. "I won't. I promise. Thank you."

He nods.

I bite the inside of my cheek and glance at the others over his shoulder, then walk out of the room.

"What the fuck are you doing with that girl, Brother?" I hear Jericho ask before the door closes behind me.

25

EZEKIEL

"Are you fucking her?"

I slowly turn to face my brother.

Jericho is on his feet. He takes a deep breath as we step toward each other. "Are you?"

Robbie makes a whistling sound and I see his eyebrows shoot up while he keeps pounding on the keyboard.

"I don't see how that's any of your business," I tell Jericho.

"She's a little young, isn't she?"

"Remind me. How old was Isabelle when you put a baby in her belly?"

He narrows his eyes. Truth isn't fun sometimes. "And apart from that, she's got shit on you that can land you in prison. She blackmailed you, which is how you met, in case you forgot. And I'd bet my ass she's lying about those missing files."

He is right about all those things. I didn't miss how she scratched her nose on her shoulder when she said she didn't know where the external drive was. But I'm not about to tell my brother that.

"Whether or not I'm fucking Blue is irrelevant." I take a step toward him.

He takes one to meet me. "I beg to differ."

"Explain to me how my sex life is of any significance to you, Brother."

"It's of significance if it can get you in trouble. Your judgment is clouded, Zeke. I see it. I'm sure Robbie here sees it."

"Whoa, whoa, keep me out of your sibling rivalry."

"This isn't fucking sibling rivalry. This is my brother needing to get his head out of his ass," Jericho says to Robbie or to me, I'm not sure. He stands there studying me for a long moment. "Helping her won't bring Zoë back," he says, tone a little gentler.

"Why is everything I do about Zoë?"

"Isn't this about her? Isn't you saving Blue some sort of atonement for having failed to save Zoë? And by the fucking way, that wasn't your job. And her death wasn't your fault. It was our father's. That's the end of that story."

I take a minute. I need it to get the swell of emotion under control. I only speak once I've collected myself. "Blue is not Zoë. End of story," I say, my voice low. "If I want to fuck her, I'll fuck her. Quite frankly, it's none of your business. Also end of story."

"She's trouble. I'm telling you—"

"You think I don't know that?"

"Do you know that?" he asks, eyebrows so high they disappear into his hairline.

"Boys, boys, sit down. Look at this." Robbie turns the laptop around and Jericho and I both glance at it. "This is Wyatt Hoxton."

Jericho resumes his seat and I walk around behind the sofa to look at the laptop on Robbie's lap.

"Who the fuck is Wyatt Hoxton?" Jericho asks.

"Mugshot. I remembered seeing that tattoo more recently and I'm thinking this might be the man Blue saw."

He zooms in on the photo and behind Wyatt's long hair I can just make out part of a tattoo that looks like the coda.

"Who the hell is he?" I ask.

"Wyatt Hoxton is a part of the special guard for the Councilors of the Tribunal. That is what your illustrious court system is called, is it not?"

The Tribunal is IVI's legal arm. Operating outside and independent of the legal systems set in place in various countries where we are present, IVI has a government in and of itself. Society members, most of whom are born into the world and a few, like us, have bought into it, are subject to the laws created by and for Society members. We are protected but also held accountable, in a different way than your average run-of-the-mill citizen.

"You're saying he was the man who came for the laptop? And nearly raped Blue?" I ask, my brain adding on the fact that she was sixteen at the time. "And what about the one-handed mystery man?"

"That I don't know. The few files I found buried deep within the laptop might suggest whoever our friend Lucky was working for was either a Society member or someone who was collecting information on members. This one here, De La Rosa, one of the founding families, isn't that right?"

I nod. "Santiago is head of his family. His father and brother were killed a few years ago. He has a sister, Mercedes. She's married to Judge Montgomery."

"Mercedes has been a bad girl."

"What do you mean?" Jericho asks.

Robbie sets the computer on the coffee table and gets up to pour himself a whiskey. I take the seat he vacated, and Jericho and I read.

"What the hell?" Jericho says.

"She killed a courtesan?" I scroll down the page and continue to read. There is a photo of the murdered woman and some backstory on her. The woman was not Society but worked at The Cat House as a courtesan. Mercedes's family is powerful, even within The Society, and when she was brought to face The Tribunal, it was all hush-hush, apparently.

"It's written like a fucking journal entry."

Jericho nods and we continue to read. "Judge Montgomery initiated the Vicarius clause. What the fuck is that?" he asks.

"He took responsibility for her actions. He'd have taken whatever punishment was decreed," I say.

"Fuck." Jericho sits back, rubs his eyes. "Twenty-four lashes. Remind me what fucking year this is?"

I look up at Robbie who is standing watching us. "Is this some sort of blackmail file?"

"Looks like it."

"Are there more on the laptop?"

"I'm guessing one of the Councilors recorded these. I put a folder on the desktop. It states not only the outcomes of several trials at The Society but also suggests there are visual recordings of the sentences being carried out. Medieval punishments from the sound of things."

"These aren't official court papers." They're not written that way. These are kept with emotion. Relish, even.

"I believe these would be the unofficial versions. I wonder if Lucky hacked into one of the Councilors computers and got his hands on these."

"How would he even know about IVI's existence?"

"That's the tricky part. The gun is registered to IVI. Someone from inside hired him to get this information. Wyatt works for the Councilors. I wonder if they found out and sent Wyatt to retrieve the laptop once Lucky was arrested. All I know for sure is it all points back to The Society. If you find that external drive, I can try to get into the files. See if we can pinpoint where they came from," Robbie says.

"Blue mentioned the mystery man looking for the laptop. And she mentioned her father was afraid of whoever he was working for," Jericho says.

"You think he was keeping his end of the bargain and delivering? Saving his ass?"

Jericho shrugs a shoulder.

"Can we get into his bank records, see if he was paid?" I ask.

"I'll see what I can do," Robbie says.

"Could also be someone else hired Lucky and the Councilors found out. Sent Wyatt to retrieve the laptop," I say, trying to think it through. "Either way, Lucky was working for someone. He wouldn't know about the existence of IVI or The Councilors to even know to look for this otherwise. And then the Councilor or Councilors found out. So there are potentially two sets of players within IVI."

"Either way, at least one person knows our father's death was no accident," Jericho says.

I nod.

"I don't trust she's telling the whole truth, Zeke."

"Oh, I know she's not," I say.

He seems surprised.

"She has a tell when she lies. She knows where the external drive is."

"Does she know who commissioned her father?" Jericho asks.

"I don't think so."

Robbie sits down, closes the lid on the laptop. "Not much more I can do without the drive."

"Let's confirm first if Wyatt is the man who was at her house," Jericho says. "Then we'll know if the Councilors are involved.

"How?"

"Isabelle and I are attending a charity dinner at The Society tomorrow night. I'll add two to the table."

26

BLUE

Zeke tells me the following day about the charity dinner taking place at The Society that night. I'm not exactly thrilled by the idea, especially of potentially seeing the man who attacked me, but it's the only way to know for sure if it was him which will tell us something about who wants what my father stole.

This whole thing is a little insane. The fact that the gun was registered to IVI, that it is someone from inside this creepy secret society who'd hired my father to steal whatever files he stole. It's a lot to take in.

"I need something from you," I say to Zeke once we're finished discussing the event.

"What's that?"

"I need you to move Wren and Rudy."

"I have guards stationed—"

"I'd feel better if she was somewhere new. Someone could have followed us to the care facility. I saw you checking the rear-view mirror after we left them and, well, I'd rather not take a chance with her. You said you'd help us. I'm asking you to help."

It takes him a minute, but he nods. "Where?"

"There's another facility nearby. It's called the Margaret Stone Center. It's supposed to be good."

"I've heard of it."

"Do you think we could get her in there? And Rudy as her private nurse? Could you get that done, I mean, you being a St. James and all," I say that last part loftily.

"I'll see what I can do."

I nod. Thank him. The day passes remarkably slowly and, in the evening, when I return to my room from wandering around the house, I find a stunning black satin corset gown hangs on the back of my bedroom door. Soft feathers line the low bodice, and the dress is cut to accentuate every curve. The skirt is split high along the front of one thigh and a pair of heels with feathers matching those on the dress sits on the floor. It's all very beautiful and also very much not me. At least nothing I've ever worn before or could imagine myself in, but looking at it, it makes me want to put it on.

"Your hair wasn't blue when you were sixteen, right?" Zeke asks as I gently brush my fingers along the delicate feathers, the soft satin.

I shake my head. "I dyed it when I got to New Orleans. I don't think he'd recognize me. I was a late bloomer so I looked like a kid. What about Craven or any of the men from The Cat House seeing me?"

Zeke shrugs a shoulder. "Let them." He checks his watch. "Get dressed. We'll leave in half an hour."

"Are you sure this is a good idea?"

"You'll be safe." His phone rings and he walks out of the bedroom to take the call, closing the door behind him.

I pull the dress off the hanger, lay it on the bed and strip off my clothes. The tag is still hanging on the dress. It's from an exclusive boutique I have walked by once or twice in town. One of those places I'd definitely feel awkward to walk into. My eyes bulge when I see the price. Did he buy this for me? For one night? Did he spend this much money on such an impractical dress?

"Rich people." I shake my head but there's a part of me that's pleased. That's excited to put the dress on. To wear the heels and to feel beautiful.

I catch a glimpse of my reflection in the mirror over the dresser, take in my short, blue and black hair, the scar that is not quite invisible although well camouflaged.

I am not beautiful. And this is not a date. I need to remember that. I strip off my things and slip the dress over my head. It's a perfect fit, as I knew it would be. He has a good eye for size. The cut of the dangerously low bodice accentuates my breasts, pressing them from beneath to make them swell over the top of the dress.

A small clutch that matches the dress sits beside the shoes and I pick it up, dig the flash drive out of my jeans pocket and stash it inside.

In the bathroom, I reapply my makeup, paying extra attention to the scar on my cheek. That's one way Wyatt, if it was him, might recognize me. Although it was bandaged then. I apply thicker eyeliner than usual, dab matte crimson lipstick on my lips and, since all I have are a few pins, arrange my hair in a sort of messy up-do which, coupled with the collar and the neckline of the dress, isn't bad actually. Not elegant, not Society, but not horrible.

The bedroom door opens. I brush a lock of hair that's too short to be pinned behind my ear and walk into the bedroom, weirdly nervous about him seeing me like this.

Zeke is looking at his phone, so I have a moment where I get to take him in unobserved. He's dressed in a tuxedo. He is elegant. He was born elegant. Black on black, he looks exactly like the anti-hero he is. Dangerous. Dark. And so fucking sexy I'd like to climb him.

Fuck.

I shake my head.

What the hell is wrong with you, Blue?

Zeke looks up. Our eyes meet and, for a moment, we stand just like that, staring at each other. He appears taken aback and I'm first to look away, feeling the heat of a flush creeping up my neck to my face.

He recovers himself more quickly. I forget how much more experienced he is than me. "Dress looks good on you, Blue," he says, approaching.

I don't have shoes on yet, so I feel shorter than usual and have to crane my neck back to look at him.

"You too," I say, not quite meeting his gaze.

He raises his eyebrows.

"I mean the tux. It looks good." God. I'm an idiot.

His eyes narrow, one corner of his mouth curving upward. I take in the sharp edge of his jaw, the neatly kept five o'clock shadow. I breathe in aftershave as he touches the collar at my neck, then dips his hand into his pocket and produces a small lock of brightly sparkling fine crystals—at least I think they're crystal because it can't be diamonds, surely. He attaches it to my collar.

"And," he starts, and from that same pocket he pulls out two dangly earrings, also crystal I guess. "The earrings are on loan," he says. "Don't lose them."

I take them from him, put them on, and try to act casual as I cross the room to pick up the shoes. I slip the strappy things on my feet. They're uncomfortable but so pretty. I catch a glimpse of myself in the mirror over the dresser once more and, for a moment, I just take in the reflection of myself, of us when he comes to stand beside me.

We look like a couple. A good-looking couple, actually. Like we fit.

Zeke's eyes meet mine in the mirror. My gaze falters. He's too experienced, too confident. A man who knows what he wants.

I clear my throat, step away. "Do people in your world often spend a month's salary on a dress they'll wear once?" I ask, disrupting whatever was happening.

"That's not a month's salary for people in my world," he says with a wink. "One thing." He pulls me close by my hips, and, eyes locked on mine, slips his hands under the dress.

"What are you doing?" I ask, capturing his forearm.

"Panty lines," he says, dragging my panties down and off.

"I'm not going without—"

He backs me against the table, lifts me to deposit me on top of it. "You're nervous."

I nod.

"Relax," he says and, keeping his hands on my pelvic bones, crouches down between my legs, pushing the dress up, my legs wide. He sets his hands on either side of my sex and, with his thumbs, draws me open. He looks up at me with a dark, hungry look in his eyes.

With that he closes his mouth over my pussy, and I gasp. My hands come to his head, weaving into his hair as he licks the length of my pussy. I close my eyes and moan when he circles my clit with his tongue, then nibbles it with his teeth.

"Oh God. That's." He closes his lips over the nub then and sucks and oh my God. His mouth is so warm, his tongue so wet and him sucking on my clit like he is takes me over the edge in seconds. I close my thighs, hugging his head to me and press myself into his face, moaning as I come, biting my lip so hard I taste my own blood.

When it's over, and my knees are wobbly, he straightens, holding me up as I stand. He looks down at me with a satisfied grin on his face.

"What was that?"

"Me helping you relax."

I nod, in some stupid trance as I shudder, coming down off my high.

"You taste good," he tells me, helping to steady me once I stand. "Sweet."

"Thanks, I guess?" What am I supposed to say to that.

"Ready?"

"Don't you want to, um, brush your teeth or something?"

He laughs outright. "I prefer your taste on my tongue."

"Okay then." I shake my head, unsure what to make of this, of him, and wipe my palms on the sides of my dress. "Oh. One sec." I hurry to the nightstand where I left my phone and unlock it. I make a weird face and snap a selfie, noticing how flushed my cheeks are. I start a knock-knock joke to Wren, telling her I'm going to sleep and will tell her the punchline in the morning. I put the phone into the clutch. "Ready."

Zeke sets the light cashmere wrap around my shoulders and we walk into the hallway, down the stairs and out the front door where Dex is waiting by the Rolls Royce. I'm nervous. I don't know why. It's not like I care that I will probably stick out like a sore thumb. I have a feeling Society folks can smell an interloper a mile away.

But as I get into the car with Zeke right beside me, I remind myself that this is not a date. We're going to see if Wyatt is the man who broke into my house to steal the laptop. Because that will answer some questions although it will undoubtedly raise new ones.

What will I do if it's him? If he's the man who tried to rape me. Rape. God. I shudder at the memory. My heart races and that ringing starts in my ears.

Zeke puts a hand on my knee as if he senses my nerves. His skin is warm, his hand solid.

"Steady, Blue."

I nod, unsure how he realized where my head had gone. I'm safe, I remind myself. I'm not sixteen anymore. And I'm with Zeke and he's not going to let anything happen to me. He promised me that and I believe him.

"So do you know everyone there?" I ask once the shrill pitch in my ears settles into a low, manageable hum.

"Know them and don't like them. Not that they like me or my brother much. I don't give off warm fuzzies, remember?"

"Why don't they like you? I thought you were all, I don't know, connected or bonded or something through your Secret Society secretness."

He snorts. "Our Secret Society secretness?"

I shrug a shoulder. "Brethren?"

"Well, for one thing, my family, the St. James's, were not born into The Society. We bought our way in."

"Wait, what?"

"We bought our way in. Well, my father did."

"You can do that?"

He shrugs a shoulder. "When you have enough money and enough hate you can do anything." His eyes go flat momentarily before he blinks and shakes his head. He turns to me. "You don't slip away tonight, you understand?"

"Yes, sir," I salute.

"I mean it."

"Believe me, I don't hope to run into Wyatt Hoxton on my own ever again. Hell, I don't even want to run into him with you there."

"My brother's wife, Isabelle will be there. I think you might actually like her."

"As opposed to your brother?"

He grins. "Jericho can be difficult."

"No!" I feign shock.

"You like me better than my brother then?" he asks, and I think he regrets it the moment the words are out. I don't know how to answer but just then, we pull into the

IVI compound along with a string of expensive Rolls Royce's. My anxiety rises as the car slows to a stop. Zeke climbs out and Dex opens my door as Zeke walks around. He extends his hand to help me out.

I take it, step out into the breezy night. I tug my wrap closer and look around. We've entered on the courtyard side. I'm used to the employee entrance of The Cat House which is not front and center. We step past the line of cars and through the gates into the courtyard. It's huge, the walls surrounding the compound high. Several trees are hung with lanterns and it's almost as though the entire area is lit by thousands of candles and the stars in the sky. Flowers add drama at every turn, and the sound of a violin comes from inside the double French doors that stand open. Waiters circulate with trays of champagne, and I wonder what is housed within the buildings. The one I do know, one I heard rumors about in my time at The Cat House is behind me. It's the circular Tribunal building. I turn to glance over my shoulder and shudder at the imposing shadow it casts. A small window high up, one of few, is the only one with light burning inside.

"Is that really... I mean, do they have trials and... things there?" I ask Zeke.

He nudges me forward. "And things," he says to me then turns to Jericho. "Brother."

Jericho reaches us, nods to Zeke and turns his untrusting gaze to me. Beside him is a stunning woman who is smiling wide, her face bright and open and welcoming. The absolute opposite of her husband.

"You must be Blue," she says, coming to give me a hug.

An actual hug.

I'm so taken aback, it takes me a moment to hug her back. The St. James family are not huggers.

"I'm Isabelle," she says, pulling back, but keeping hold of my hands.

"My wife," Jericho says, his voice dark as he wraps his hand around the back of her neck. Is that a St. James thing?

Isabelle glances at him. "I think she probably got that, Captain Obvious."

He narrows his gaze at her, tugs her close. The action is, in a word, tender, and I can see the affection between them. He whispers something into her ear that makes her blush.

She clears her throat and blinks several times.

From the satisfied grin on Jericho's face, he got the last word on that one.

Zeke leans toward him and says something I don't hear.

"How are you doing over there at the house?" Isabelle asks after clearing her throat.

"Okay, I guess." Does she know exactly how I came to be at the house?

She looks over her shoulder at Zeke. "He's not so bad," she whispers. "More bark than bite."

"I'm not so sure about that," I say. "He has plenty of bite." My face burns as I realize how literal that is even though that wasn't my intent.

Isabelle doesn't seem to catch on, though. "He should come to the house. Angelique would love to see her uncle. She adores him. I don't see why all this secrecy—"

"Isabelle," Zeke interrupts. He smiles down at her, kisses her cheek. "You look lovely, as usual. I understand congratulations are in order."

She glances at her husband, flushes and sets a hand on her stomach. "Thank you. We're excited."

Oh. She's pregnant.

A waiter comes carrying crystal flutes of champagne. I take one. Zeke doesn't.

"One of those sparkling water?" Jericho asks.

"Yes, sir," the waiter says and turns the tray slightly. Jericho takes the glass and hands it to Isabelle but doesn't take a drink himself.

"Do my eyes deceive me?" a woman's voice carries across the courtyard. The waiter disappears into the crowd.

Zeke groans beside me.

"Christ," Jericho mutters under his breath.

Isabelle giggles.

"Is that you, Ezekiel St. James?"

We all turn to find three women, I'd say all in their mid, maybe late-twenties, approach. They're decked out in designer everything, all swaying hips and boobs and heels too high for anyone to be able to do anything but sit and look pretty. And pretty they are, beautiful, without a doubt. Their leader, the tallest of the trio, pours herself against Zeke and kisses his cheeks three times.

Are we in fucking Europe?

I'm tempted to grab his arm or something but manage to keep my hands at my sides. I remind myself that he's not my boyfriend. This isn't a date. Instead, I watch, and

I'm sure my expression shows exactly what I'm thinking which is WTF?

"Vivien," Zeke says, not even attempting to pretend to smile.

"How long have you been away?" she asks, pulling back but holding onto his arms, her claws curled around his biceps. Is she feeling him up? I'm the one he just ate out, I remind myself but then wonder why the fuck I am jealous. "You know I tried to look you up when I was traveling through Amsterdam. Figured I'd stop to see an old friend on my way to the French Riviera, but you never returned my calls!"

"Didn't I?" Zeke asks, bored.

The women who flank Vivien glance at me then at their leader. "Viv, looks like Ezekiel brought a friend," one says.

All three turn their attention to me. These women are not friends. Or I guess they're what you'd call frenemies? I don't know, this is not my world. The ice in their eyes as they take me in, looking down their noses at me, lets me know exactly what they think of me. I usually don't mind my height, but this is when I wish I were taller so at least I wouldn't have to look up at them.

"Aren't you going to introduce us?" Vivien says, turning her gaze to Ezekiel, her smile wide, all bright, shiny, too-perfect veneers.

"No," Zeke says, and I can't help my snort and apparently, Isabelle can't either and she turns away, pretending to clear her throat.

The women glance at Isabelle, giving her pretty much the same hateful glance as they did me.

A gong chimes and I jump.

"Excuse us," Zeke says. He wraps his hand around the back of my neck exactly like his brother had a moment ago with his wife and we turn to follow Jericho and Isabelle into the procession heading to the double French doors.

"I think she likes you," I whisper to Zeke.

He squeezes my neck. "She's a viper."

"She's pretty."

"If you like snakes."

"Her boobs alone—"

"Careful. I might think you're jealous," he says, giving me a dark glance he replaces quickly with a generic smile to someone who greets him.

"Not jealous. But I am curious if you've fuc—"

He turns to me. "Women like that are utterly uninteresting to fuck." The line comes to a stop, and I almost crash into Isabelle, but Zeke tugs me backward in time.

"But have you?" I ask, turning to him, seeing Vivien and her friends watching me from where they're still standing.

Zeke's gaze follows mine before returning to my face. "She sucked my dick once. Exactly once."

"Oh." Why am I bothered? Why would I care?

"It was years ago. I was drunk. That was the end of that. I did not fuck her. I had no intention then of fucking her and have no interest now. Anyway, it doesn't matter. I'm fucking you now. I don't bed hop. And besides," he leans in close. "I can still taste you on my tongue."

I flush hot and red and look around. I'm pretty sure the couple behind us heard that.

Zeke chuckles. Before I can say anything, the line begins to move again, and he nudges me forward. I don't know what I think about what he just said. It's strange. Unsettling. But a glance back at the glamorous, beautiful, confident Vivien does do something to me. I am none of those things. And on top of it, she's Society. She belongs here, same as him. I do not.

Jericho drops his hand from Isabelle's neck to her lower back and I gasp because her dress is cut low and her hair, which is twisted into an elegant braid over her right shoulder, leaves her back fully exposed. There, along her spine, is a tattoo. Two dragons intertwined. A smaller version of what I saw on Zeke's back. I glance at Jericho's hand, see the ink that matches Zeke's. Do they both have the same tattoo? Is it some sort of family thing? Isabelle's is beautiful. Much smaller than on the men. It's intricate and utterly gorgeous.

We enter the large ballroom and people disperse to find their tables. I look around, taking in the mirrored walls, the ornate paneling, the crystal chandeliers hanging from the ceiling, their light reflecting off floors polished to a high shine. Large round tables are draped with floor-length tablecloths in cream, breathtaking bouquets of deep red flowers drip from tall centerpieces upon each. There are more plates and silverware than I can count and several bottles of wine on each table. A twelve-piece orchestra plays something vaguely familiar, and I gather from the dance floor, which is empty now, there will be dancing later. Along a side wall, long tables are set with expensive looking items. A silent auction, I guess.

We reach our table and Jericho pulls a chair out for Isabelle. Before anyone can decide where to put me, I pull out the one beside Isabelle and sit.

"The Councilors," Jericho says to Zeke.

They both turn and Isabelle and I follow their gaze to where, not too far from where we are, three men enter. One is much older than the other two who look to be in their late forties or early fifties.

"Who are they?" I ask Isabelle.

"The first is Councilor Montrose, he's the oldest. Councilor Hildebrand is next, and Councilor Augustus is the last one. He's holding the cane which is for show, mostly."

Following them are four men, two who stand beside the door from which the three entered. They clasp their hands in front of them and I can see they're security from their posture, the way they move, the way they take in the entire room.

More guards follow, and just before the door closes, he enters. I gasp. Because all of a sudden, just like that, I'm back in that little broken down house and I'm sixteen years old and he's there. That man. On top of me. His hand inside my panties. His gun in my hand.

EZEKIEL

Blue has gone white.

I turn from her to the man she's staring at. Wyatt Hoxton. He's built as tall as me, but thicker. He's solid, if a little overweight. I imagine him lying on top of Blue, crushing her. How she'd have felt trapped beneath him. Could she breathe? Then, when he put his hand down her pants—that thought makes me ball my own hands into fists and blood boils in my veins. The monster inside me stirs, urged by a blood thirst. I wasn't always like this. I never backed away from a fight, but rarely did I seek it out. Now, it's as though I know what will happen. What I'll do. And I'm anxious to get to it.

"All good, Brother?" Jericho asks.

I blink, draw a deep breath in and turn to him. I nod.

His gaze moves from me to Hoxton.

I'm glad when Isabelle touches his knee to draw his attention and I return my attention to Wyatt Hoxton. His hair is so blond, it's almost white and his eyes are so pale that when his gaze scopes the room, I see the pinprick of black pupil scan every face.

It's when his gaze pauses in our direction that I think we made a mistake. I think Blue might be wrong.

Because I think he might recognize her.

"Look at me," I say to Blue who turns to me, so she is facing away from him. My eyes are on Hoxton. His move to me. Does he sense danger? Does he know yet that he will die tonight? My heart thuds slow and heavy against my chest until Hoxton's gaze moves past me, expression unchanging. If he registered my animosity, he did not show it. When Montrose calls his attention, he leans down, and I see the tattoo Blue mentioned. The coda at his neck.

The Councilors make their way to their table at the front of the banquet room. It's set on a dais for the three men. Men who, with a word, can destroy a life. Can snuff it out entirely.

"Can we go?" Blue asks.

I turn my gaze down to hers. Her eyes are huge, face pale. The pulse at her neck is throbbing.

"Not yet. It would draw attention."

"But—"

"Relax. He didn't recognize you," I say, but it's a lie. I know it because even as the Councilors settle into their chairs, Hoxton's gaze returns to us. Settles there.

Blue picks up her glass and downs the last of her champagne. Councilor Montrose, the oldest of the Councilors, clinks his fork against his glass and the instant he does, the room goes quiet.

Hoxton remains behind Montrose. In my periphery I

see Jericho shift his gaze from Hoxton to me. I meet my brother's eyes.

What does this mean, if a guard of The Tribunal was at Blue's house to retrieve the laptop? Did Lucky steal information from the Councilors? Was he paid to do it? The entries, were they kept by all three? I don't think so. These were personal entries. Did the Councilors then learn what had happened, that personal files were stolen, and, learning it was Lucky, send Hoxton to retrieve the information?

Like Hoxton, I let my gaze move over the faces in the room. Powerful men, these. I see Santiago De La Rosa with his wife, Ivy. Beside him is his sister, Mercedes, a woman capable of murder. She is now married to Judge Montgomery, who took her punishment onto his own shoulders, literally. What scars does he hide beneath that bespoke suit he wears?

Was it one of the men in this room who hired Lucky to steal the information or was it someone outside of IVI. My gut says inside. It's what makes the most sense. And there are so many possible motives.

Greed. Money. Blackmail. Vengeance.

I shift my gaze to Blue. She's clutching her bag in her hands, her eyes wide, but distant. She has the flash drive. I know that. She lied about not knowing about it. Did she retrieve it when she retrieved the money I found in her pocket? Was it there, all along, inside the pocket of her dress and I didn't think to look?

And what does she plan to do with it? She has accepted my protection for herself, for her sister. Why not give up the flash drive? Unless it's her backup plan. Does she know who wants it? If she thinks handing it over to whoever hired Lucky to steal it or to the Councilors will buy her freedom, she's wrong. Dead wrong.

Making someone like Blue disappear is an easy task for anyone in this room.

Montrose finishes his speech. I only realize it because the room breaks out into applause. On Hildebrand's signal, the orchestra begins to play and several doors swing open to allow dozens of waiters to enter carrying trays of food, and dinner begins.

28

BLUE

I'm not sure how I make it through a starter and the main course. My plate goes back mostly untouched. Zeke sits beside me cutting into his meat, eating. I'm not sure he tastes anything though. His energy is tense. Muscles tightly bunched. When he looks up from his plate, it is in one direction.

The head table.

The man standing guard behind the Councilors.

Before dessert is served, there is a break, and couples begin to make their way to the floor to dance a waltz. I watch, wondering if they all go to the same dance school or something because everyone seems to seamlessly fall into place, as if the whole thing were coordinated.

The Councilors leave the room, their guard with them. Hoxton doesn't look back and I feel myself relax. I look to Zeke who is finishing the last of his wine.

"Can we go?"

"Soon," he says. How does he manage to look so

relaxed, I wonder. No, that's not it. It's not relaxed. It's something else. Like he's decided something.

"I need to run to the lady's room," Isabelle says, wiping her mouth with her napkin.

"I'll come with you," I say, pushing my chair back.

Zeke's hand closes round my knee. "No."

"I need to pee."

"I'll take them," Jericho says, standing.

Zeke finally nods, although he's reluctant. I get up and Isabelle and I walk side-by-side, Jericho at our back. Jericho waits outside of the lady's room, and we enter.

"What's going on?" Isabelle asks me as soon as we're alone.

I wonder how much she knows. How much her husband has told her. I don't want to lie to her but am not sure how much I can say.

"I'm pretty sure you're picking up the same vibe I am from them. Did you notice no one at the table said more than two words to us?" she asks.

"Zeke is charming like that," I say with an eye roll.

Isabelle smiles, takes out her lipstick. "I know what brought Zeke back," she says, keeping her eyes on her reflection in the mirror until she's done, then turning to face me. An older woman walks into the powder room and Isabelle says hello to her, then takes me aside. "Jericho doesn't want to upset me, given the baby and all, but I'd feel better knowing."

I nod. She has a right to know. "I think one of the men guarding the Councilors may be connected to my father. I'm not sure how much you know about that, but basically, it's bad news if he is."

She studies me, a wrinkle forming between her eyebrows. "How bad?"

"Bad."

There's a knock on the door and we both turn when someone pushes it open and clears his throat.

A man.

I grab Isabelle's wrist and push her behind me. If it's him, if it's Wyatt Hoxton, I won't let him hurt her.

But I exhale a sigh of relief when Jericho's head comes into view. He sees us, takes in my hand around his wife's wrist. Isabelle steps around me.

"You're leaving. Dex is outside. He'll take you to the car," he says.

"What about you?" Isabelle asks.

He glances at me. "I'm going to get Zeke."

"Where is he?" I ask.

Jericho's jaw tightens and he shakes his head once.

"Did he go—"

"I don't know," Jericho cuts me off, glancing at his wife.

I look at her, then him. My heart races. Did he go after Wyatt?

"Let's go." Jericho says and holds the door open.

Isabelle steps out and I follow her. Dex is standing nearby. The gong chimes and people begin to pile back into the banquet room.

"I left my wrap," I say.

"I'll get it," Jericho says. "Dex."

Dex nods, and gestures to us to walk ahead of him.

Jericho wraps a hand around the back of Isabelle's neck and draws her close. They look at each other, forehead to forehead, and it's so intimate a moment, I feel like I should look away. "Zeke and I will take my car," Jericho tells her. "Don't worry. I'll be home soon."

"Okay," she says, and I can hear that she is worried.

I look around for Zeke, trying to find him in the crowd as the gong goes again.

"Come on, Blue," Isabelle says weaving her arm through mine and leaving me no choice but to leave with her, Dex following close behind us.

29

EZEKIEL

I slip out of the ballroom after the Councilors do. The three men head toward a private room at the end of the corridor where another of their guard stands waiting at the door.

"Are you back for good?" a woman asks, stepping into my line of vision.

I turn toward the sound to find Vivien whatever the fuck her last name is. At least she's on her own. Her minions aren't flanking her.

"Excuse me?" I ask.

"Are you back home for good?" she asks, trying to sound flirtatious but clearly irritated likely at my earlier dismissal of her.

"Why?" I ask, shifting my gaze around her when the door opens to glimpse the backs of two men. The Councilors disappear inside. Hoxton and another of the men stand guard outside.

She takes a step to the right, placing herself squarely between me and my line of vision to the door.

"Just wanted to know if you were back so we could pick up where we left off."

I furrow my brows. "I didn't realize we'd left off anywhere."

"I mean," she starts, tilting her head to one side, pushing her hip out in the opposite. She licks her lips suggestively and I have a vague memory of her kneeling before me, but that's where it ends. Like I told Blue, I was drunk. Very drunk. That or maybe she just wasn't very good.

Vivien reaches out to adjust my bowtie. I raise an eyebrow.

"You know, Ezekiel, we were getting to know each other and—"

I take her hands and move them off my person. "You're wasting your time, Vivien. I'll be very clear. I'm not interested."

She seems stunned by this, and I imagine it's not often she's turned down. I suppose technically, she's beautiful but like I told Blue, she's a viper. I assume most men tuck tail when she approaches.

"You can't be interested in that girl you brought." She snorts. "I mean, that hair. And is she even Society? I've never seen her around."

A gong chimes and from behind her, the door opens, and the Councilors emerge. In my periphery, I see Vivien's posse approaching, pointing. I guess she'd slipped away.

"Your friends are coming," I tell her. "If you don't want to be humiliated, I suggest you walk away and don't approach me again. Not interested. Never was.

Never will be. Not sure how to make that any clearer."

"Viv! You sneaky thing! Did you steal her away *again*, Ezekiel St. James?" One of the women giggles, giving me a flirtatious poke on the chest.

"She's all yours," I say and extricate myself.

Wyatt Hoxton separates himself from the other two guards and turns down a staff corridor. The gong chimes once more, the halls thinning out. I follow Hoxton, watch him slip through the last door. I think about him on top of Blue.

Think about him putting his hands on her.

Touching her.

I push the door open and enter. It's a staff men's room with lockers along one wall, stalls along another, and a long, mirrored counter with sinks opposite the door I just entered through. Apart from the occupied stall where I can hear a man taking a piss, the room is empty.

I lock the door.

A toilet flushes and Hoxton steps out of the stall. He does a double take.

"You can't be in here," he says.

I glance down as he finishes tucking himself back into his pants. For a big guy, he has a small dick. But most men like him do. It's why they're such assholes.

"This is a staff room." He walks to the counter, and rather than washing his hands, he picks up a comb and runs it through his hair.

"You should wash your hands, you know. Says so, right there. Employees must wash hands." I point to the sign.

He glances at it, then at me, pale blue eyes narrowing in his fat face.

"You're with that girl. With the blue hair."

I narrow my eyes, study his features.

"Do we have business?" He sets the comb down and turns fully to face me.

"We might."

He cocks his head, watching me. "What business would that be?" He shifts his gaze down to my hands, then back to my face. "Ezekiel St. James."

The tattoo. Jericho and I have identical tattoos. It's common knowledge.

"What business do we have?" I ask. "I guess I have a question for you." He raises his eyebrows. I step toward him. "What makes you think it's okay to shove your dirty, unwashed hands down a sixteen-year-old girl's pants?"

"What the fuck are you talking about?" he asks, and for a moment, I wonder if I got it wrong. But then, his expression changes. I see the instant it all clicks into place. Not that it matters, because I'd already decided I was going to do what I'm about to do. Whether or not he remembered what he did to Blue is irrelevant.

Hoxton's face morphs, that mask of civility that was barely there dropping, the monster beneath surfacing. He reaches around back, under his jacket. I expect a gun, but he draws out a switchblade instead, pushing a button to release the knife and stepping toward me, his violence practiced.

But I'm no stranger to violence. When he slashes the knife through the air an inch from my face, I duck backward and grab his wrist. He's strong, but so am I. And I have much more rage inside me than any one man should.

I keep hold of his wrist, slamming it against the mirror, hearing the glass crack, watching it splinter.

Blood from the back of his hand spills into mine and I do it again, slamming it hard enough to knock the knife out of his grasp. It clatters off the counter and drops to the floor.

He doesn't need it though. This man knows how to fight. But so do I.

He slams a fist into my gut, and I stumble backward, but I'm up fast, dad taught me that, taught me to swallow the pain or there'd be more. Pussies always got more. A rage I haven't felt in a long, long time takes over, that beast within wide awake and given free reign, autonomy over my body, my limbs not my own, but belonging to this thing. This animal inside me.

The killer inside me.

We're on the floor. I taste blood, my own possibly. His? Likely. I pummel my fist into Hoxton's face. He's gotten soft, fat.

"Tell me. Tell me why you'd think putting your filthy hand inside a sixteen-year-old girl's pants is acceptable. Precursor to your little dick following? Is that it? You like to rape little girls, you fucking pig? You fucking filthy, disgusting pig."

He laughs and it throws me off. Something isn't right. He fights back but he's no match for my growing rage. For my years' worth of fury. When his fingers close over the switchblade just above his head and bring it up to my face, I take hold of his hand and twist it, turn it, and, looking into his beady, evil eyes, I plunge the dagger into his gut.

Blood spurts across my face, covering my hands, my clothes. It's warm and bubbling and Hoxton's eyes are wide as he coughs once, twice, blood gurgling in his throat as I thrust the blade upward, cutting through flesh and fat and guts, disemboweling the bastard, feeling his life drain from him, spill all around him, the stain of it permeating every sense until all I see is red. All I smell is blood. All I want is blood.

A familiar sound breaks into the moment.

I sit back, drag in a breath. Try to make out what the sound is. I know it.

It's my phone ringing in my pocket. I don't reach for it, and it stops. I look down at the man before me. Arms and legs splayed. Head to one side. Eyes open. Blood trailing from his mouth, his gut.

"Fuck! Zeke!"

I look back at the door just as it slams open, and Jericho crashes inside the splintering frame.

He takes in the scene. I follow his gaze. Get to my feet. I walk to the sink and switch on the water. Jericho closes the door. It won't stay though. It's busted, the frame ripped apart.

I wash my hands, Hoxton's switchblade clattering loudly against the porcelain sink.

"What the fuck did you do?" Jericho asks.

"He recognized her. It was a matter of time," I say, tone calm. It's mostly true.

"Jesus Christ. Look at you." He looks down at Hoxton. No need checking for a pulse. He's dead. "Stay here. I'm going to get the car. There's an exit at the end of the corridor. Where's your phone?"

"Pocket."

"When I call you again, you fucking pick up. Stay. We don't need anyone seeing you like this." He vanishes and I bend to wash my face, my heart rate normal again. I push water into my hair. It's sticky with blood. I look down at Hoxton and feel much the same as when I killed my father and his mistress. Nothing. Not a damn thing.

When the door opens again, I turn to find my brother stepping inside holding a trench coat.

"Put this on," he says, and I take it from him. "Let's go. We have to leave him."

I take the switchblade from the sink, close it and casually tuck it into my pocket.

"Did anyone see you?" Jericho asks as he checks the corridor before we step out and walk swiftly down the hall to the exit. We step outside, cool night air feeling good against my skin.

Sirens wail. I pause. Did someone already call the police?

No. That makes no sense. We're The Society. We have our own police.

We climb into my brother's car. "Where are Blue and Isabelle?"

"Dex is taking them home. Did anyone see you?" Jericho asks again.

"I don't care if they did," I say.

"For Christ's sake." He drives out calmly, exiting the compound.

Those sirens grow louder, lights flashing in the distance, traffic building.

"What the fuck was that? What are you, some sort of fucking vigilante now?" Jericho asks.

"I told you he recognized her. It was a matter of time before he put two and two together. We shouldn't have brought Blue here. That was a mistake."

"At least we know now. Hoxton would be working for the Councilors. One of them sent him to Lucky's house to get those files. And I have a feeling it was them who intervened to get Lucky out on parole so early into his sentence. They want those files back. We need to find them."

"I'll get it."

He looks at me, eyebrows furrowed. "How?"

"She has it. I know she does. I'll get it tonight." I draw my phone out of my pocket to call Blue as our car slows to join the building queue. There's an accident up ahead.

The phone rings. Did she bring it with her to the event? Yes. She put it in her bag. I remember that.

"What the fuck?" Jericho says.

I look over at him, disconnecting when the phone just keeps ringing. He opens his door. I shift my gaze up, out of the front windshield.

"Isabelle?" I hear him ask.

I open my door, but this doesn't make any sense. Isabelle is here?

"Isabelle!" Jericho runs toward the accident scene.

I look at the car that's been hit. The airbag that's been deployed. I'm out and running before I can make sense of what I'm seeing.

30

BLUE

My head. Fuck. My head.

I squeeze my eyes as my ears ring, the pitch blocking out all other sounds. I hear a groan and I try to open my eyes.

Someone screams and a car alarm goes off. Drivers honk their horns, angry? Why? Why all this noise?

My door opens and I fall backwards out of the car. Someone catches me. I was wearing my seatbelt. I'd just put it on. Hadn't I?

We got into the car, Isabelle and me. Dex closed the door and climbed into the driver's seat, silent, as usual. I saw a lipstick on the floor I recognized. I bent to get it, realizing it was the car Zeke had used to kidnap me. Yes. That's it. I unclipped my seatbelt to get the lipstick. We were at the light. It was just for a second.

But then, something hit us. Hard.

Isabelle.

Oh, God. Isabelle. She's pregnant.

The moaning. I think it's her. I try to pry my lids open, but it's impossible.

Hands grip my arms hard. I'm hauled out of the car. Fingers dig into my flesh. My head flops backward, my legs slap onto the pavement, dragged, hard gravel cutting into the backs of my legs before I'm lifted, held against what feels like a stone wall. It's in that second I manage to open my eyes. Just for the briefest of moments. Just for a split second.

And what I see.

Oh God. No. No.

It can't be. What I see, it makes no sense. He's at the compound. He's guarding the old men. I saw him. I know I did.

He grins and his mouth stretches into a too wide smile, and I realize it's not his mouth. He has scars, lines that go from the corners of his mouth to his ears. They make him look like a clown. He didn't have them that night. My mind would have cataloged it, wouldn't it?

"Remember me?" he asks, his voice familiar, his breath hot and foul on my face.

I stare up at him, those blue eyes so pale they're almost colorless except for the pin prick pupils.

I struggle and he chuckles.

"Good."

Ambulances arrive at the Rolls Royce. Dex is passed out. I glimpse his big body slumped forward. God. Is he okay? And there is Isabelle. Isabelle looks dazed. She's crying. Screaming?

The baby. Is the baby okay?

Oh God.

We're out of the commotion, heading away from the flashing red lights.

"No!" I scream, animated, swinging my arms, my legs as the hulk with those terrifying eyes, his hair cut shorter, his face fuller, drops me into the trunk of a car. He glances in the direction of the commotion, then turns to me and smiles that clown-like smile again.

"Looks like we'll get that chance to be together after all. And I owe you, you little bitch."

He slams the trunk shut, trapping me. A moment later, I'm hurled against its edge as tires screech taking a hard turn away from the sounds of sirens and safety and an absolute, suffocating darkness swallows me.

THANK YOU

Thanks for reading *By Sin To Atone*, the first installment in the Sinners Duet.

Blue and Zeke's story concludes in *By Blood To Avenge*.

ALSO BY NATASHA KNIGHT

Sinners Duet

By Sin To Atone

By Blood To Avenge

Heroes & Villains Duet

The Heroes We Break

The Villains We Make

The Augustine Brothers

Forgive Me My Sins

Deliver Me From Evil

The Sacrifice Duet (IVI)

The Tithing

The Penitent

Ruined Kingdom Duet

Ruined Kingdom

Broken Queen

The Devil's Pawn Duet

Devil's Pawn

Devil's Redemption

To Have and To Hold

With This Ring

I Thee Take

Stolen: Dante's Vow

The Society Trilogy (IVI)

Requiem of the Soul

Reparation of Sin

Resurrection of the Heart

The Rite Trilogy (IVI)

His Rule

Her Rebellion

Their Reign

Dark Legacy Trilogy

Taken (Dark Legacy, Book 1)

Torn (Dark Legacy, Book 2)

Twisted (Dark Legacy, Book 3)

Unholy Union Duet

Unholy Union

Unholy Intent

Collateral Damage Duet

Collateral: an Arranged Marriage Mafia Romance

Damage: an Arranged Marriage Mafia Romance

Ties that Bind Duet

Mine

His

MacLeod Brothers

Devil's Bargain

Benedetti Mafia World

Salvatore: a Dark Mafia Romance

Dominic: a Dark Mafia Romance

Sergio: a Dark Mafia Romance

The Benedetti Brothers Box Set (Contains Salvatore, Dominic
and Sergio)

Killian: a Dark Mafia Romance

Giovanni: a Dark Mafia Romance

The Amado Brothers

Dishonorable

Disgraced

Unhinged

Standalone Dark Romance

Descent

Deviant

Beautiful Liar

ABOUT NATASHA KNIGHT

Natasha Knight is the *USA Today* Bestselling author of Romantic Suspense and Dark Romance Novels. She has sold over a million books and is translated into seven languages. She currently lives in The Netherlands with her husband and two daughters and when she's not writing, she's walking in the woods listening to a book, sitting in a corner reading or off exploring the world as often as she can get away.

Write Natasha here: natasha@natasha-knight.com

NATASHA KNIGHT

www.natasha-knight.com

Made in the USA
Las Vegas, NV
06 December 2024